"I think you caught me off guard again," he whispered.

"Is that a bad thing?"

"No." He straightened, and Laura finally gave him the space he needed by releasing him and crossing her arms in front of her. The sun hadn't come up yet on this blustery February morning, and her skin was suddenly awash with goose bumps. "But I'm not sure what to make of it yet. You're not..."

"Lisa?"

"I just never thought..." His shoulders lifted with an apologetic shrug. "It was always her."

She nodded her reluctant acceptance of the facts. "And I remind you of her. That kiss was a trip down memory lane for you."

"No. You're not anything like her. That kiss was nothing like anything she and I ever shared."

But Lisa was the sister he'd loved. She wasn't anything like the woman he loved. "It's okay, Conor. I've just always...wanted to kiss you." That much she would confess. "I knew you'd be good at it. We're cool, though."

He didn't look entirely convinced.

DO-OR-DIE BRIDESMAID

USA TODAY Bestselling Author

JULIE MILLER

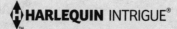

Thank you to my readers who were so kind to help me figure out Conor
Wildman's story. I needed a few details on the fly, and you found them
for me. I appreciate you taking the time to find the answers I needed from
Protection Detail and getting back to me so quickly. You're the best!

To Anu-Riikka Henriksson, Jeriann Fisher, Kathy Brown, Kay Singletary,
LaJuonna Sirk, Danielle DePierre, Mary Birchwood Lawson,
Lanita Idrus, Diana Roman and April Fowler.

ISBN-13: 978-1-335-64066-6

Do-or-Die Bridesmaid

Copyright © 2019 by Julie Miller

Recycling programs
for this product may
not exist in your area.

Printed in U.S.A.

www.Harlequin.com

Julie Miller is an award-winning *USA TODAY* bestselling author of breathtaking romantic suspense—with a National Readers' Choice Award and a Daphne du Maurier Award, among other prizes. She has also earned an *RT Book Reviews* Career Achievement Award. For a complete list of her books, monthly newsletter and more, go to juliemiller.org.

Books by Julie Miller

Harlequin Intrigue

Rescued by the Marine
Do-or-Die Bridesmaid

The Precinct

Beauty and the Badge
Takedown
KCPD Protector
Crossfire Christmas
Military Grade Mistletoe
Kansas City Cop

The Precinct: Bachelors in Blue

APB: Baby
Kansas City Countdown
Necessary Action
Protection Detail

The Precinct: Cold Case

Kansas City Cover-Up
Kansas City Secrets
Kansas City Confessions

Visit the Author Profile page at Harlequin.com.

CAST OF CHARACTERS

Conor Wildman—This KCPD detective's sarcasm is a line of defense he's built around his battered heart. When he attends a wedding, he's reunited with the girl next door. But Laura Karr isn't a freckle-faced teenager anymore, and he struggles to reconcile their lifelong friendship with the desire he feels. When a killer targets her, he becomes Laura's personal protector. But is he willing to risk his heart again?

Laura Karr—Although her friendship with Conor feels as familiar as ever, she's always wanted something more. But her project to get Conor to see her as a grown woman is derailed when her best friend is murdered. When key evidence falls into Laura's hands, the murderer sets his sights on her. With a killer in hot pursuit, do Laura and Conor have any chance at a happily-ever-after?

Chloe Wilson—When Laura's friend turns up dead, her questionable choices become Laura's problems, too.

Isaac Royal—How jealous can this mild-mannered accountant be?

Vincent Orlando—Chloe's boyfriend swept her off her feet with money, romance and promises he might not be able to keep.

Marvin Boltz—Vincent's attorney.

Deputy T.J. Cobb—Is his good-ol'-boy charm covering up something sinister?

Prologue

The honor of your presence is requested...

"You've got to be kidding me." Conor Wildman skimmed over the details of the wedding invitation. Embossed pink hearts and lilac ribbons adorned the paper and the little RSVP card. This had to be a joke. Only it wasn't.

It took a lot of gall for his ex to invite him to her wedding.

It took even more gall for said ex to be marrying his former best friend.

But he wasn't bitter. Conor snorted the hot coffee he was drinking up his nose and cursed. Yeah. That was about how good he felt at reading Joe and Lisa's names linked together—like a hot, black brew scalding his sinuses.

He should have left yesterday's mail sitting on the counter and come back to it after work this evening. Better yet, after a drink after work this evening. No. He should have dumped the pale pink envelope in the trash and then skipped straight to the drink after work at the Shamrock Bar where he and his new friends at KCPD often hung out after hours.

That was why there'd been no return address on the envelope—so he wouldn't automatically trash it. If it wasn't pre-coffee time in the morning, he might have thought to check the envelope for the Arlington, Virginia, postmark. But since he'd just come from the shower and poured himself his first cup, he'd been blindsided by the reminder of all he'd lost these past two years.

It didn't matter that he logically understood why Lisa had dumped him—too many necessary lies, too many absent nights with his former job at WITSEC. Dumped was dumped. There was no logic that could ease the pain of being told he wasn't good enough, he wasn't right enough to make a good husband to her.

It wasn't the first time he hadn't been enough to make someone stay.

He was no longer with the US Marshals service, no longer in Virginia, no longer brooding over the life that had been denied him. But a wedding invitation?

There was no one in his life who'd be sending him a Valentine this February. Had he hoped he'd picked up a secret admirer? That his mother had arranged for someone to send him a missive before her death eight months ago? She'd known the breast cancer was winning, that it had metastasized beyond any hope of saving her. She'd spent a lot of those last few weeks getting her affairs in order, trying to get his life shipshape, too, knowing she was the last of his family. Had Marie Wildman been in collusion with his ex's mother? The two women had been friends for as long as Conor had been alive. Had his mom asked the Karr family to keep an eye on her only child? Make sure he was happy?

If so, what was the point of inviting him to a weekend wedding extravaganza back home? A torturous weekend trapped in awkward conversations with well-meaning friends and painful memories wasn't his idea of fun. There was a reason he'd moved halfway across the country to take an assignment in Kansas City, Missouri. A reason why he'd left the Marshals Service to become a cop with the KCPD instead of moving back to Arlington after his assignment in KC had wrapped up.

Lisa Karr had rejected his ring and said he wasn't the kind of man a woman who wanted a normal life should marry. Hell, she'd quoted some statistic about how a man with his temperament and job skills would be divorced in a couple of years if they'd gone through with their engagement. He didn't think either Lisa or Joe Gerhart was the rub-our-noses-in-Conor's-pain kind of cruel. But he could see them doing a favor for his mom, feeling sorry for him. Poor Conor. *We didn't mean to hurt you. We know it's been a tough year. We want you to know we will always care about you.*

It didn't matter that Lisa had officially broken up with him before she'd started dating Joe. It still felt like his friend had stolen his girl. Knowing the two had kept the relationship quiet while he'd been dealing with his mom—seeing them together for the first time at Marie's funeral—felt like Lisa had cheated on him.

It made no sense, but that was what he felt. He'd been one raw emotion, keeping it together for so long that he wasn't sure he knew what he felt anymore. Except pissed that Lisa and Joe had invited him to their wedding. In one week. Like he was a problem they needed to fix.

Conor considered taking another hit on the hot liquid caffeine he lived on. But he wasn't that much of a masochist. He carefully set the mug down on the kitchen counter and stepped away to finish dressing.

Striding into the bedroom, he dropped the towel cinched around his lean hips and pulled on his shorts and slacks. The white shirt with the button-down collar came next. He crossed to the mirror over the dresser and combed his short, wheat-blond hair into place before looping a tie around his neck. He stopped mid-Windsor knot and eyed the brown-and-navy stripes before pulling it off and tossing it onto the bed.

Lisa had given him that tie.

He'd settle for the solid blue tie with the tiny food stain on it. That would have driven her nuts. She'd fuss over his incompetence when it came to dressing himself before catching on that it was just a ploy to get her to put her hands on him. Then they'd laugh. And there would undoubtedly be a kiss.

Conor tugged that tie off, too. Nope. Better opt for the completely neutral, no-history-involved tie he'd picked up at a Christmas party.

He'd once been amused by Lisa's tendencies to have the details of her life arranged so that there were no surprises. His inability to guarantee her that home-for-dinner-every-night predictability was one of the reasons she'd broken off their engagement. The possibility that he might not come home at all one day because of the inherent dangers of working in law enforcement had sealed the coffin on their future together.

But he couldn't give up his job—couldn't surrender the gun and the badge and the crazy hours he'd once worked as a US marshal, tracking down fugitives and protecting witnesses. He wouldn't give up the man he chose to become after the father who hadn't wanted him or his mother had abandoned them. He couldn't give up who he was. Not even for the girl he'd loved since college. His promise that she would always come first in his heart hadn't been good enough for her. She needed a sense of security that his gun and badge couldn't provide.

Ironically, now that she was no longer a part of his life, he'd resigned from the Marshal Service. His last case guarding a witness relocated to Kansas City had made him question too many of his supervisor's decisions. If his boss didn't have his back, and wouldn't put the woman he'd been protecting first, then the oath he'd taken—Justice, Integrity, Service—meant nothing. Conor had lost too much for his work and his life not to mean anything.

He thought Lisa had understood that. That she accepted his job was a big part of who he was as a man. But maybe she'd been in love with a version of him he just couldn't be.

He understood Joe and Lisa's need to mend fences and make the past right, so they could move on with their future—to their new life. But why was their happiness *his* problem? He slipped his holster and badge onto his belt, grabbed his suit jacket and headed back to the kitchen.

Conor finished off his tepid coffee in one long

draft. He shrugged into his jacket and picked up the wedding invitation to toss it into the trash.

That was when the note that had been tucked inside fell out and drifted to the tile floor. Conor's shoulders lifted with a wary sigh before he stooped down to retrieve it.

He unfolded the handwritten note—with messages from both Joe and Lisa.

Con—If I was marrying anyone else but Lisa, you'd be standing by my side as best man. I let this go because I know you've been dealing with your mom this year. But it's killing me that you aren't a part of our lives anymore. Hell, Lisa talks about how much she misses the three of us hanging out the way we did in college so much that I'm getting a complex. I finally told her to send you an invitation. Bail me out, bro. Lisa needs to see you're okay with her own eyes. Come to the wedding. Do it for yourself, too, and show everyone here that you're okay.
—Joe.

He flipped over the paper to Lisa's flowery handwriting. What was this? An intervention to help him get over how sucky they thought his life had become?

Dearest Con—I know things ended badly between us. Deep down in your heart, you know I couldn't make you happy in the long run, nor you me. But we were friends long before we were something more. We were practically family. Marie and Mom were like sisters. Your mom would want you to be happy, not stewing in anger or grief or whatever it is that is keeping you away from home.

If you don't care about me or Joe, then think of your mother. We all miss her. Mom most of all. Seeing you here, representing Marie, would make her so happy.

You may think there's no one in your life who worries about your well-being. But we do.

I hope we can be friends again. I'd love to have a big brother like you in my life. Please come. We miss you.

Yours truly,

Lisa.

Big brother? He hadn't felt brotherly toward Lisa since she'd sprouted breasts in middle school.

Brotherly was what he felt toward Lisa's tomboy little sister, Laura. The squirt always seemed to be around when he'd come over to hang out with Lisa, and she'd even tagged along on a couple of dates in college. He'd taught her to swing a softball bat and spit watermelon seeds from the tree house that hovered over both their backyards. Laura had freckles and braces and snorted through her nose when she laughed. Lisa was feminine right down to her painted pinkie toes. Not in any universe could he equate *brotherly* with his feelings for Lisa.

But his heart hadn't been enough. *He* hadn't been enough.

He wasn't sure he could handle the friendship she wanted. The pain of her rejection compounded by his mother's death, the guilt of not seeing how unhappy she'd been with him, wouldn't allow friendship to flourish again. But maybe he could give Lisa one day.

Show everyone here that you're okay.

"You played me like a fine violin, Joseph." Shaking his head, Conor scooped the invitation up and stuffed it into his pocket. His decision was made.

Time for a road trip to Virginia.

Chapter One

The Methodist church was packed with enough guests that Conor could easily slide into the last pew without drawing attention to his arrival.

He'd convinced himself that taking a few vacation days and driving to Arlington for Joe and Lisa's wedding was a necessary thing. It was a matter of pride to show them that he wasn't so grief-stricken about his mother's death or wounded by Lisa that he was too weak or vulnerable to wish them well.

So, here he was, in the flesh, back at the church where services for his mother had been held, the same church the Wildmans and the Karrs had attended growing up. Detective Conor Wildman was doing just fine on his own, thank you very much.

But he wasn't going to make a spectacle of himself. He might be proving that he was a gracious loser, that he had made the right choice to move on, but those emotional scars were still fresh.

One of the hazards of standing six foot three, though, was that blending in wasn't always an option. When Joe walked in from the waiting room beside the altar with his best man and a groomsman—one a fraternity brother he recognized from college, the other probably an accountant friend from work—he adjusted his dark-rimmed glasses on his nose and looked again, letting Conor know he'd been spotted. Joe beamed at seeing Conor in the back row near the exit. Conor offered his former college roomie a thumbs-up and a wry grin.

But when Joe took a couple of steps to come down the aisle toward him, Conor shook his head and pointed to the back of the church, reminding Joe of his priorities as the organ music finished with a dramatic flourish. The best man pulled Joe back into place, rubbing Joe's shoulders and teasing him about putting the kiss-the-bride stuff ahead of the "I dos," which sent laughter through the pews like a wave.

Conor didn't laugh. The organist began playing the overture to the traditional processional. But he wasn't ignoring the joke or appreciating the music so much as he was distracted by the sudden shuffle of commotion in the narthex just outside the sanctuary's open doors. From his vantage point he could turn and see what the fuss was about while the congregation buzzed with chatter, waiting for the grand entrance of the bridal party.

"Put down your cell phone." That terse whisper would be Lisa. Something wasn't going according to her no-doubt meticulous plan for the day. Conor's chest expanded with a steadying breath at hearing her voice again. He knew all her tones and what they represented. That one was her nervous-that-everything-is-about-to-fall-apart-but-I'll-cover-my-fear-by-sniping-at-someone-else tone. "If she chooses not to be here to oversee the guest book, then…why isn't Chloe here?"

"I don't know. She isn't answering. And no one's seen her here at the church, either." Since Conor didn't immediately recognize the second woman's voice, he tilted his head to get a glimpse of pink tulle curving over a generous flare of hips. Tulle and satin gave way to pink lace clinging to some very nice breasts that rose and fell with a huffy sigh. But bangs of short brown hair with caramel highlights and a netted glittery pink feathered headpiece pinned above her ear obscured the woman's face. "I'd like to know where my friend is, too. Do you think Isaac knows?"

"Don't go out there and ask him," Lisa chided. "He's already at the altar with Joe." All he could glimpse of her was the hem of her lacy white gown as she paced beyond his line of sight. "I don't care if she's leaving me in the lurch. I care about you being the first one down the aisle."

"Relax, dear. Aunt Sandra handled the guest book just fine." Conor smiled as a familiar face joined the woman in the pink bridesmaid dress. Lisa's petite mother and his own mom's best friend, Leslie Karr. "Please, sweetie. It's time. We can't start the ceremony without you."

Sweetie meant one of Lisa's sisters. And since her older sister was as tall as Lisa, that meant the frilly pink bombshell was her younger sister, Laura. Um, *bombshell*? Conor remembered braces and blue jeans and tennis shoes. He never would have ogled Laura the way he'd been assessing her figure a few seconds earlier, and, in fact, would have gone all big brother on any guy who did let his eyes linger on her curves for that long. She was just a kid. Well, the Laura he knew had been like a kid sister to him.

But the attitude was familiar.

"I'm here, aren't I?" Laura protested. "You told me to find Chloe, and now I'm concerned because I can't."

A pregnant belly draped with more pink satin and tulle moved into the picture, blocking his view of Laura and her mother. Linda Karr-Colfax moaned and rubbed at the small of her back. A similar clip of feathers dangled from her upswept hair. "Mom? Ty was playing with my hair. Is this thing still in okay?"

"I thought we checked everything before leaving the dressing room," Lisa scolded, while her mother secured the gaudy thing in Linda's hair. "And do not have your baby today."

Linda chuckled at her middle sister's worry. "Take a deep breath, Lisa. They're Braxton Hicks contractions. I've had them with all three babies. And neither of the boys came early." She muttered something slightly less reassuring when a little boy in a black tuxedo somersaulted into the picture. Linda's attorney husband followed with a sleeping toddler on his shoulder and pulled the boy to his feet. Linda brushed the dust off the tiny tux's shoulders. "You only have to wear this for a little while, Timmy. Just until we take the pictures after the wedding. Where is your pillow with the rings tied to it?"

"Has he lost it?" Lisa's long dress swirled into the tableau, but again his anticipation at seeing the beauty he'd loved was thwarted by the angle of the doorway.

Laura knelt in front of her nephew to hand him the embroidered white pillow. "Not lost. Here." The little boy chortled with delight. Now that he had a clear view of that part of the lobby, Conor saw that there was a toy truck tied to the pillow, too. "You hold tight to that, and you won't lose that pillow again, will you."

Appeasing the youngster in the face of all the tension happening out there made Conor smile, too. "Nice move, Squirt," he murmured under his breath, automatically thinking of Laura by the nickname he'd given her growing up.

But her smile faded a split second before she looked down at her phone and pushed to her feet.

More than noticing that she'd snipped off her long pigtails for a short, angular cut that hugged her jawline and played up the waves in her high-lighted hair, and had traded her braces for a sweet, mischievous smile, he registered the frown lines that deepened beside her green-gold eyes. Baby Sister was really worried about something.

She texted something in response to the message she'd received.

"Laura! Phone!" Lisa pleaded.

"Sorry." Laura turned it off and slid it beneath the lace of her gown to tuck it inside the sweet-heart neckline.

"Seriously? You'll ruin the look of the dress with that thing sticking out of your cleavage."

"Like I don't look like a piece of cotton candy, anyway."

"Mother!"

Leslie Karr had handled bigger spats than this with her patient tone and knowing smile. "Laura, sweetie, let me put your phone in my purse." With another lift of her bare shoulders, Laura did as her mother asked. After tucking the phone into her clutch purse, Leslie cupped her youngest daughter's cheek. "You look beautiful today."

Then Leslie turned, gently touching Linda's belly as she smiled up at her oldest daughter. "*You* look beautiful."

When she reached for Lisa, stepping out of Conor's line of sight to hug her middle daughter, his breath hitched with a mixture of anticipation and anxiety at the thought of glimpsing Lisa again. But unless he leaned out into the aisle, making his presence more than obvious, he'd have to wait like every other guest to put eyes on the bride.

"Sweetie, you look beautiful. Joe is the luckiest of men. Take a deep breath." Conor had always admired how Leslie had kept her three daughters in line. Such different personalities. Different activities all through school. Different emotional and parental needs. A little diplomacy, a little bargaining, a little bit of cajoling. But then she barked an order, and all three women snapped to attention, falling into line behind the young ring bearer. "Now. Everyone smile. Ron? Take your place. Here we go."

Conor turned away from the scene in the lobby and finally found a reason to chuckle. Leslie Karr had a little bit of five-star general in her, too. He recognized that tone from his own mother's bag of tricks when it came to raising him. His mom and Leslie had been such close friends—they'd probably traded parenting secrets.

Leslie walked down the aisle on the arm of an usher, followed by Tim Colfax and his son, the ring-bearer making vroom-vroom sounds as he carried the pillow by the truck.

Then he saw Laura. The moment she stepped into the sanctuary, their eyes met. Her mouth rounded with a startled O of surprise and he winked. The blush on her cheeks deepened to a rosy hue and her megawatt smile lit up the church. Yeah. The tomboy of the family had sure grown up. She made cute work on her compact, curvy frame. She fluttered her fingers in a friendly wave before hurrying over.

"Hi." Those same fingers curled around his neck and she leaned in to kiss his cheek. "I'm glad you're here."

"Hey, Squirt."

Just as quickly as she'd kissed his cheek, she stepped away and fell back into line. She made a face and tapped her cheek, indicating he check his own face, before heading slowly toward the altar again.

Conor dutifully pulled out his handkerchief and wiped at the mark she'd left, leaving a smear of rosy pink lipstick on the white cotton. He was glad someone here could elicit a genuine smile from him. He folded the handkerchief and returned it to his pocket, letting his gaze follow Laura down the aisle.

Her cotton candy dress swirled around her calves, drawing his eyes down to slim ankles and strappy high-heels she wouldn't have been caught dead in back when she'd been in middle school, hitching a ride with him to school activities before she could drive. Conor leaned back in the pew to do a little bit of math. Those memories had been from a decade ago. Laura had to be about twenty-five now, five years younger than him. She'd been at college when his breakup with Lisa had happened, and he'd moved away. He recalled now that she'd sent flowers and a heartfelt condolence letter to his mother's funeral, but she hadn't attended because something with work had kept her out of town. He'd have remembered the swing of those hips and that wire-free smile if he'd seen Laura recently. All grown up. Sharing little resemblance to her taller, willowy sisters beyond the changeable hazel color of her eyes.

He traded a smile with Linda when she entered the church. He pointed to her belly and whispered congratulations. Then the music changed and everyone in the congregation stood.

Conor buttoned his jacket and held his breath,

waiting for that gut-check of recognition when he saw Lisa on the arm of her father. They paused for a moment at the back of the church. She was an elegant vision of sparkles and lace in her figure-hugging white gown. Yes, she was beautiful. But seeing her gaze seeking out Joe at the front of the church, her taut expression relaxing into a genuine smile, did more to bring closure to their relationship than her returning his ring ever had.

Hell. She didn't love him. Not anymore. Certainly not the way he'd loved her.

He must have been scowling at the thought because when their gazes finally met, Lisa hesitated. She mouthed, "Are you okay? We'll talk later."

She was that worried about him? He wasn't so hard up that he wanted a woman to settle for him just so he wouldn't be alone in the world. If Lisa wanted Joe, she should be with Joe. He was man enough to accept that. Conor smiled before he doffed her a two-fingered salute and waved her on down the aisle to the man she loved.

And then she walked away from him. Again.

Where was the knife to the heart he'd been expecting? The fires of jealousy burning through his veins? He'd been so certain he needed to come here to save his pride, to prove to everyone in his old life he could be happy and successful without their interference, that the confusion he felt now was a little unnerving. As the guests sat and the ceremony started, Conor admitted he was melancholy that their long history had been tossed aside, his planned future altered.

But he wasn't angry.

His mother's illness and truly accepting that he and Lisa were never going to be left him feeling…empty.

Great. Understanding was a humbling thing. He hadn't needed to prove anything to anybody but himself by coming here today.

But now that he'd admitted the truth, skipping out the back of the church was hardly an option, unless he wanted to start some real gossip or face more heartfelt letters of concern for his well-being. Just like a stakeout assignment, he was here for the duration of the ceremony and reception.

But he had a bad feeling that today was going to be a lot longer and more stressful than any stakeout.

"ARE YOU TALLER?" Conor smiled at the warm greeting and wound his long arms around tiny Leslie Karr, treasuring the maternal hug at his waist. "Conor Wildman, I think you're taller. I'm not shrinking, am I?" Keeping one arm linked around his waist, Leslie turned to her husband beside her in the reception line. "Ron, am I shrinking?"

"No, dear. You're as petite and perfect as always." Ron Karr seemed to be taking the demands of the day in his familiarly patient stride. Probably a life skill learned from raising three daughters. He extended his hand. "I'm glad you could make it, Conor. It's good to see you again, under happier circumstances."

"Yes, sir." Conor shook hands with the father of the bride. "Congratulations, Ron. How are you two holding up today?"

"Fine." His forehead wrinkled with concern. "We should be asking you that question, though."

Leslie patted Conor's stomach, tsk-tsking between her teeth. "You're thinner, though. Are you eating well? Taking care of yourself?"

"Yes, ma'am."

"He's fit, Les, not skinny." Ron patted the cummerbund of his tuxedo. "I'm the one you need to be fattening up." At six feet, Ron Karr towered over his wife, but he still had to look up to meet Conor's gaze. "She's got me on some crazy diet where I eat weeds and straw five nights a week. She hasn't baked me a pie in six months. Trust me, once it's cut, I am diving into that wedding cake."

"Oh, stop," Leslie chided over the men's laughter. "The doctor said we both needed to cut down on sugar and red meat." She tilted her chin back up to Conor. "I promised your mother I'd keep an eye on you. Of course, I don't know how I'm supposed to do that with you being a million miles away."

Conor grinned at the exaggeration. "It's only eleven hundred miles."

Leslie frowned. "Is it really that far?"

"A couple days' drive. Or one really long one."

"You must be exhausted."

He hugged her shoulders, silently reassuring her that he'd passed his KCPD physical with flying colors, and that she didn't need to honor the mom code of perennial worry. Not on his behalf. "I got in yesterday. I'm staying at Mom's house. There are still a few things to go through there, some repairs I need to line up before I put her house on the market."

Leslie's sigh was audible. "You're selling Marie's house? You're not coming back? Ever?"

Come back to what? Constant reminders of all he had lost here in Arlington? His old boss was here. Lisa. Memories of his mother. Even the ancient scars from his father. Still, Leslie's stricken expression reminded him of those last days with his mother in the hospital. One of Marie Wildman's regrets was that she'd never see her grandchildren.

"Conor, you will *have children? You'll have a family?"*

He'd gently squeezed her frail hand and promised, telling her whatever she needed to hear to ease her worries and keep any last bit of strength she had for herself. Back then he'd been gutted by Lisa's rejection. All he had left was the precious life slipping away in front of him. *"I will, Mom. I promise. One day, I will."*

"Don't wait forever." Marie's hand had trembled in his. *"Life isn't always what you expect it to be. It's been just you and me for a long time. And now I'm leaving you all alone. I wish I could be at your wedding. I wish I could see my grandchildren..."*

"Mom—"

"I don't regret a moment. I've been happy. I've lived a wonderful, fulfilling life. I want the same for you." Even though her energy was flagging, there was a smile on her gaunt face. *"I've always been so proud of you. My brave son risking his life for others. I don't want you to mourn me forever. You live your life. Don't you dare settle for anything. Or anyone. Lisa never understood how deeply you feel things—I don't think you even know."* She reached up to stroke his cheek. *"But I do. The right woman is out there for you. I want you to love and be loved the way the way your father and I once..."* Her voice faded away. He supposed heartache like hers never completely went away. *"Find your happiness, son. Hold tight to it with both hands."*

Life isn't always what you expect it to be...

Conor roused himself from his thoughts and smiled down at the woman who had always been like a favorite aunt to him. "I don't know my future plans yet, Leslie. For right now, though, they're in Kansas City."

Ron seemed to sense the dark turn of Conor's thoughts and pulled his wife back to his side. "Les, dear, we're holding up the line. The rest of our guests are waiting." He shook Conor's hand again. "Come by the house anytime. There's still a gate in the fence connecting our backyards. The walkway is a little snow-packed this time of year, but it's still there."

"Thanks. I'll stop by before I leave town."

Still raw from that trip down memory lane, Conor wasn't prepared for Lisa stepping out of line to hug him. For a moment, he stood there in shock. Another second gave him time to re-member the way her tall frame fit against his body, like two pieces of a puzzle joining together. A third, saner moment reminded him to pat her back instead of squeezing her tightly, and then push her away. She wasn't his to hold anymore.

"Congratulations, kiddo. You're a beautiful bride. But then, I never had any doubt you would be."

"Con—"

"Take the compliment." He cut her off before she could turn his words into any kind of apology.

"Thank you."

Dismissing Lisa to move on down the reception line, he reached out to take Joe's hand and pulled his friend in for a back-slapping bro hug. "Congratulations, man. You dress up pretty good for a numbers geek."

Joe grinned. "I can be taught."

But his intent to move past the bride and groom to greet Joe's parents was thwarted by the tug of Lisa's hand on his. "Are you happy, Con? Please be happy."

"Why is everyone so worried about my happiness?" he joked. "This is your day. We're here to celebrate you two."

Lisa's gaze darted to Joe, then back up to Conor. "We never meant for our engagement to hurt you. But I know it did. Losing your mom and then running away..." Her grip on his fingers tightened. "We've been so worried. You don't call. You don't write. Don't throw away your life here because of us."

Conor pulled his hand from hers. He schooled the irritation out of his tone. "Guess what? I didn't run away from anything. I went where the job took me. Remember? The job I'm obsessed with?" He immediately bit down on that snap of sarcasm and apologized. He was over this. He was over her. But being back in Arlington was stirring up painful memories. "You should be thinking about your honeymoon, not me. If you two aren't happy together the rest of your lives, I'm gonna come back and kick both your butts."

"No worries, man," Joe assured him, looking relieved to hear the teasing.

"Thank you. You're just so important to both of us." Lisa's next hug was a little too long and a little too uncomfortable. When he heard the telltale sniffle against his lapel, he leaned back, automatically pulling his handkerchief out of his pocket for her.

But Joe had pulled one out, too. He tucked his into Lisa's hand, kissed her cheek and suggested she take a break to powder her nose.

"Sorry about that," Conor apologized, balling his handkerchief into his fist. "That's just the way my mama raised me."

Joe nodded, looking not at all threatened by any old habits Conor might have that involved his new wife. "Heard you took up drinking."

One bender the night Lisa had dumped him, and suddenly he was an alcoholic. Conor shook his head. "Is that the rumor?" He nodded toward the doorway where Lisa had slipped out of the reception. "No wonder she's so worried about me. I swear my only vice is coffee. Strong and black."

Joe laughed, reminding Conor of the camaraderie they'd once shared. "That'll eat a hole in your stomach."

"Standard hazard of the job."

"I also heard you left the Marshals Service." Joe pulled back the front of his tuxedo to slide his hands into his pockets. "Does that mean you've found someone to settle down with in Kansas City?"

Even the accountant wasn't above interrogating him. "I'm still a cop."

"So that's a no." Joe's deceptively casual stance never changed. "It never was a competition between us. You know that, right? I would never move in on your woman. I didn't ask Lisa out until you two were done."

His breakup with Lisa didn't seem to bother Conor as much as it seemed to bother everyone else. But this big ol' pity party, expressing all this concern for his welfare, was rubbing on his last nerve. "No hard feelings, Joe. Just take good care of her. And make sure she takes good care of you."

"I will." Joe extended his hand. His grip felt firm and familiar. "Take care of yourself, too."

Conor congratulated Joe's parents and then backed out of the line, turning toward the main reception area.

"Con?" He glanced back to see Lisa hurrying to Joe's side. Her makeup was all neatly in place again as she called after him. "Save a dance for me, okay?"

Yeah. That wasn't going to happen. Thankfully, the other guests moving through the reception line demanded the bride and groom's attention. He wondered just how long he had to stay before anyone else accused him of falling apart or running away.

Longer than Conor had planned, apparently. When one of his mother's former bridge-playing friends linked her arm through his and invited him to join her and her husband at their table, he resigned himself to at least staying through dinner. But several old friends of his mother's were at the table, too, and all their efforts to "help him" soured the taste of the prime rib and mashed potatoes he'd taken from the buffet.

"How long are you going to be in town?" Mrs. Martin, one of his mom's friends, asked as he picked at his cake. "My niece just had her heart broken by a boy she's been dating since high school. I think you two might have a lot in common."

Conor set down his fork as the sweet icing curdled in his stomach. Now their concern had graduated to fixing him up with other women? "I won't be in town that long."

"I could give you her number for when you come back."

Once he sold his mother's house, he wasn't coming back. "Sorry to hear that she's unhappy.

But no, thank you." Conor pushed his chair away from the table. "Would you excuse me?" Conor eyed the patterns of foot traffic around the reception hall, taking note of the easiest route to an exit door. Maybe he could get a cup of coffee to go?

And then he spotted one of those sparkly feathered hair clips moving through the chairs and round tables, momentarily diverting him from thoughts of escape. Short, brown hair. Caramel highlights. Cotton candy-pink dress hugging womanly curves he shouldn't be noticing.

Laura Karr.

When she moved past a table where the guests were seated, he caught a glimpse of her face. Her mouth was creased with frustration as she hurried after the groomsman with the dark hair and glasses. She caught up to him at the edge of the dance floor, grabbed the back of his black tuxedo jacket and forced him to stop and face her. Although there was too much noise with the band playing and the conversations buzzing around the tables to hear anything, he could tell by their body language that it was a heated discussion.

Conor's gaze narrowed as the groomsman glared down at Laura.

Was that a lovers' quarrel? Including *lover* in the same thought as the tomboy next door jarred his equilibrium, but he could tell Laura was upset. Was that guy picking on Conor's little tagalong buddy? Giving her grief? Why was he so eager to dismiss her?

Conor's emotions had been on the fritz since receiving the invitation to the wedding. Hell, they'd probably been offline long before that, but he'd just kept himself too busy to acknowledge them. But something pinged on his that-ain't-right radar and made him curious to know why his longtime friend seemed so distressed—and why Glasses Guy was so intent on shutting her down.

Rescue. It wouldn't get him out of this place, but it might get him out of his head long enough to forget the awkward discomfort of the evening.

He strode into the crowd of guests. "I'm comin', Squirt."

Chapter Two

Laura Karr might be the one person here who'd treat Conor like the guy next door he'd always been—not like the prodigal son returning home, or some poor lost soul who needed to be saved. The groomsman smacked Laura's hand off his sleeve, and Conor hurried his steps to reach her.

Smacked her?

Uh-uh. *That* wasn't gonna happen.

Conor came up behind Laura in time to hear a parting shot from the curly-haired man. "Don't mess with things you don't understand."

Over the top of that glitzy pink fascinator, Conor locked his gaze on to the dark eyes behind the man's glasses. "Hey, Squirt." He settled his hand at the nip of Laura's waist, alerting her to his presence so he wouldn't startle her, but also warning the other man that she had a friend who'd intervene if the argument turned any uglier. "Is there a problem?"

Laura's frown transformed into a bright smile

when she faced him. "Conor. I was hoping we'd get a chance to connect before you ran off."

Great. Not her, too. "I came to the wedding, didn't I? Even brought a gift. I'm not running anywhere." He kept a friendly grin on his face, ignoring the fact that moments earlier he'd been sizing up the room for his best chance to do just that. Run.

"Sure, you weren't." A heavenward roll of her green-gold eyes told him she wasn't fooled by either the words or the grin as her arms went around his waist in a welcoming hug. But he barely had a chance to complete the hug before she pulled away to stop the other man's retreat. "Isaac, wait." She tugged on Conor's hand and pulled him forward to make introductions. "I want you to meet a friend of mine. Detective Conor Wildman, this is Isaac Royal. He was Joe's groomsman today. They work together at the accounting firm."

The man who'd walked Laura back down the aisle at the end of the service blinked rapidly behind his glasses. "Detective? You're a cop?"

Conor arched an eyebrow at the dumb question. "Generally, that's what the word means."

"Conor's with the Kansas City police," Laura explained. "He moved to Missouri a couple of years ago."

Since this seemed important to Laura, Conor

extended his hand when the other man didn't. "Isaac. Nice to meet you."

Isaac Royal was clearly agitated about something. Did he have a reason not to like cops? Maybe he was just anxious to get away from whatever Laura had been pestering him about. His palm was sweaty when he finally reached out to shake Conor's hand. "You, too." He pulled away, adjusting his glasses on his nose. The corner of his mouth hitched up with a smile. "Heard what happened to you with Lisa. Women can be a bitch, right?"

Not the opening to a polite conversation Conor had been expecting. He bristled to his full height. "And some guys can be jerks," Conor pointed out. "Whatever you two were arguing about, you'd better not be referring to Laura. And if you touch her in anger like that again, I will—"

"He won't." Laura stepped forward, not needing his defense because, apparently, Isaac's snide remark hadn't been about her, after all. "Give Chloe a chance to explain herself. Call her. She's been absent all afternoon and evening. Aren't you the least bit worried?"

"Let it go, Laura," Isaac warned. "This is between her and me. Chloe made her choice."

"But Lisa was counting on her. What if she's counting on you? To save her?"

Isaac's laugh held zero humor. "I'm done being

her boyfriend when it's convenient for her. I'm not picking up her pieces. That woman is not going to hurt me anymore." Isaac excused himself, taking a shortcut across the dance floor and exiting into the hallway where the restrooms were located.

Feathers and bangles bounced as Laura fumed beside him, visually drilling holes through the archway where Isaac had disappeared.

Still clueless as to the source of the tension, but not liking how it affected his childhood friend, Conor sought some answers. "Everything okay? Do I need to have a man-to-man conversation with Mr. Royal?"

The set of her mouth was still tight even as she joked about his concern. "Just like you had a conversation with Scott Swearingen when I was in the eleventh grade?"

"A guy doesn't tell a girl he can *do better* when she asks him to the prom." Since no one had asked her, Laura had bravely taken the initiative and asked a boy to go with her. There were less cruel ways to say no than to belittle her for her not being the most popular girl in school. "I heard you crying up in the tree house that day. He was an immature jerk who hurt your feelings. What was I supposed to do?"

Laura nudged him out of the way of a row of line dancers sliding past them. "Maybe not go all big brother on his ass and embarrass me? You ambushed him in the parking lot after track practice, basically told him he was an idiot for not seeing the treasure behind my lack of boobs, straight As and wicked sense of humor."

Conor had prided himself on not throwing a punch that day. "I called him worse than an idiot. And I never once mentioned your boobs."

Although, mentioning them now, he found himself looking down at the shadowy cleft beneath the lace overlay on her gown—and just as quickly looking away the moment that most male part of him awoke with the knowledge that there was nothing teenagerish, tomboyish or lacking about Laura's curvy shape now.

"Why do you think I was embarrassed? Do you think any other boy would say yes to me, knowing you were lurking next door, waiting to pounce on them, too, if they so much as looked crossways at me?" She raised her voice as the music crescendoed to its climax. "You should have at least offered to take me to the dance yourself. Now *that* would have been real chivalry."

Conor dipped his head closer to hers to continue the conversation without shouting. Ignoring the subtly exotic scent that wafted off her hair and filled his nose, he reminded her of the facts. "I was home on spring break from college. The law frowns upon someone over twenty-one dating a high school kid. I couldn't take you."

"And I always thought that big, bad Conor Wildman was a rule-breaker. It was one of the tenets that my teenage adoration of you was based on."

He grunted a laugh at the idea he'd been any teenage girl's fantasy. "There are rules. And then there are laws. One of those, I don't break."

"Plus, there was that whole dating my big sister thing. That would have been awkward."

Yep. There was that.

She inclined her head toward the line dancers shuffling their direction again. "I'm old enough to dance with you now."

Had he imagined the hushed invitation in her voice just then?

He knew he hadn't imagined that little gut-kick of interest stirring in the pit of his stomach at that surprisingly grown-up, completely feminine tone. Conor hoped she'd been unaware of just how provocative she had sounded.

She was putting him on, right? That had always been their routine—hug, laugh, listen, tease. He was the one who was screwed up, who'd been screwed over by life. There was no way Laura's offer to dance was meant to sound like a proposition for something more. He'd been celibate and grieving, angry and heartbroken for too long to trust anything his flirt radar was trying to tell him. This was Laura. Same freckles. Same sass.

Same smile—sans the braces. The comfort in that familiarity was what he needed to focus on. Not this whole weird awareness of the pretty bridesmaid he was experiencing tonight.

Conor remembered the easy banter between him and Laura. He didn't remember any verbal innuendo or the voluptuous frame she'd poured into that candy-pink gown. And while it was a relief to find something normal about this long evening, he remembered he wasn't the only person in this conversation. There were tactics to her rambling. "You changed the subject. What were you and Isaac arguing about?"

"I'm probably being paranoid." Unlike Lisa, who fit snugly under Conor's chin, the top of Laura's head barely reached his shoulder. And that was in the heels she was wearing. Still, he had to admire that the differences in their heights didn't deter her from tilting her chin to make direct eye contact with him as she spoke. "Isaac dates a good friend of mine, Chloe Wilson. Well, he used to. They've been on-again, off-again for a year or so. She lives in the apartment above me. I introduced them."

"I take it, by the static I felt in the air between you two, that it's off again?"

Laura nodded. "Chloe was invited to the wedding, too. In fact, she was supposed to help, but she never showed. I've called and texted, but she doesn't answer. Isaac was ignoring me before the ceremony, but I finally caught up with him. He said they broke up for good this time—that she's seeing someone else. Although, I hate to think about the guy she might have dumped Isaac for."

"This new guy put up a red flag for you?"

Laura made a derisive sound that was more snort than laughter. "I wouldn't call him reliable, that's for sure. I've only met him a couple of times. He always has one or two other guys with him, like an entourage. I never spoke with any of them."

"He's a party guy?"

"If it's his own party. He shows up when Chloe's working. Makes her change plans when they don't suit him. Maybe she didn't come to the wedding out of respect for Isaac's feelings. But she'd have called Lisa or me to let us know she wouldn't be here. I'd bet money that Vinnie didn't want her to come."

"Vinnie's the new guy?"

Nodding, Laura braced her hand on Conor's arm and stretched up onto her toes, scanning through the crowd. Conor automatically followed suit, checking the diners and dancers, even though he didn't know who he was looking for. "You don't see a blonde about my size wearing ridiculously high heels, do you? I proudly accept that I'm never going to top five-three, but she overcompensates by wearing killer heels all the time. Even to run to the grocery store."

"I don't think I've seen anyone like that tonight." To be honest, he realized that he'd been so focused on his own inner demons that he hadn't paid much attention to any women younger than his late mother, besides Lisa and her sisters. A quick scan of the dance floor and dining area now didn't reveal any young blondes tottering around on scary heels.

When Laura pulled her hand away, Conor wondered at the imprint of heat that lingered on the skin beneath his jacket. What was wrong with him tonight? There wasn't anything that felt right or normal about this long-overdue trip home except for Laura. And now he was blowing this reprieve because she'd gone and grown up on him, and he couldn't get comfortable in his own damn skin around her.

"Chloe doesn't always make the best choices," Laura went on. "I worry. I mean, Isaac wasn't exactly trippin' her switch, but he was steady, nice."

The fading red mark on Laura's hand made him question what kind of temper Royal was hiding behind that geeky façade. But he'd go along with her for now. "In other words, boring. Let me guess, the new guy drives a fast car, spends a lot of money on her and looks like the lead in the newest superhero movie franchise."

Laura laughed. "You've met Vinnie Orlando?"

"He sounds like a cartoon character."

Laura butted her shoulder against Conor's arm, smiling at how he must have nailed the description of a handsome party boy who could turn a woman's head. "I guess I shouldn't be surprised that she wants to date someone else. Isaac can be a little…controlling. With his budgets and schedules. Chloe's a free spirit. She's an artist. She paints some, but mostly sculpts in clay—animals, human figures, busts. She makes ends meet by waiting tables. She's got a big heart, but she wants what she wants."

"That doesn't sound like a recipe for a successful relationship."

"I always thought it was an 'opposites attract' kind of thing for her and Isaac. She brought him out of his shell. He offered her security. Her home life isn't much to tell about. Her dad's been MIA for years, mom's in prison." Laura's sigh was audible above the pounding beat of the music. "Still, I thought she'd come today. She *is* a friend of the family."

"It's awkward when things don't go the way you planned with the person you love."

Hazel eyes swiveled up to his. "That rings a little too close to home, doesn't it? I'm sorry."

"It's not your fault, Squirt." Conor shrugged. "I'm not the man your sister needed. And try as

I might to change things, we were never going to be. I wish I'd figured that out sooner. Could have saved a few dings to my heart and my pride." He tilted his head down to her and winked. "She wants what she wants, too."

Laura's hand moved back to that spot on his arm, and Conor felt the squeeze of compassion through the layers of worsted wool and cotton he wore. Then she linked her elbow through his and leaned against his side in what he could only describe as an arm hug. When had Laura Karr become such a toucher? Or had he just never noticed that natural way she made contact with those around her before? "I'm sure today is hard for you. Lisa was so worried you'd crawled off into a dark hole after she announced her engagement to Joe. So soon after losing your mom? People here worry about you."

He was well aware of that fact. "People? You mean Lisa? She wants everything in her world to be organized, neat, pretty. Breakups aren't pretty." He nodded to the hallway where Isaac had disappeared. "Ask your friend."

The song ended and was momentarily replaced by the buzz of conversations across the reception hall before a slower tune started. Conor retreated to the nearest table, pulling Laura out of the way as dancers who weren't coupled up filed off the dance floor. Several more guests left their seats, moving forward to take advantage of the sultry jazz melody.

Laura's arm was still linked with his, the scent of her hair filling up his head, and as the crowd thinned they could nudge a little space between them again. "You and Lisa were friends long before you two were an item. We were all friends. Family, practically. That's why she was so worried."

"A guilty conscience will do that."

"Conor…"

He raised his hands in surrender, breaking the last of the connection between them, admitting that was a low blow. "Sorry. Sarcasm is my go-to when I don't know what to say. I don't know if I'm ready to be buddy-buddy again, but I'm hardly living in a dark hole."

Laura faced him. "You ran away to Kansas City."

"My job took me to Kansas City," he explained for the umpteenth time that night. "I was protecting a witness. We damn near lost her because of my supervisor's wheeling and dealing."

She was squeezing his arm again. "Is that why you changed jobs? Because you lost a witness? Is that why you stayed?"

"We didn't lose her—thanks to some help from her boss and his family, all local cops there, the Watsons and some close friends of theirs. We arrested the killer who was targeting her." The Watson family had turned out to be better allies than the unit he'd been working with at the Marshals Service. "I like KC. I like the people. I trust the friends I've made there."

"Meaning you don't trust your friends here anymore?"

"Not when they took comfort in each other's arms." For a moment, Conor wondered if the sarcasm had leaked out of his mouth again because Laura propped her fists on her hips and looked as if she was about to scold him for the uncharitable thought. Conor shook his head. The problem with old friends was that they sometimes knew him better than he knew himself.

"*People* need to stop worrying about me. I'm a grown man. I'm not drowning my sorrows in a bottle. I'm not contemplating suicide. And I sure as hell am not running away from anything. I just..." Laura's eyes darkened to nearly solid green while she waited for him to finish that sentence. "Truth? I did need some space. I couldn't think here. There were too many memories. I needed to move on, but I was drowning in everybody's sympathy and their efforts to make everything right for me again. So, when the new job opportunity came up, I took it. I don't have any regrets."

Laura's shoulders lifted with a deep breath, and

she nodded—as if someone around here finally understood why he'd left. "Loss changes you. You had a double whammy of it. You needed time and space to grieve. And you weren't going to get any better here, with us."

When he looked past the youthful dusting of freckles across her nose and cheeks, past the silly bauble in her hair, Conor could see a serene wisdom in the depths of her eyes. Maybe even a hint of sadness or regret there. Curious. "What do you know about loss, Squirt?"

Her gaze held his for a moment before dropping to the middle of his chest where she brushed away something. "Enough to know that I outgrew that nickname a long time ago."

The bride's familiar voice reached him a split second before he felt Lisa's hand at his back. "Con, are you ready to dance?"

A shiver that was part pain, part self-preservation, rippled down his spine. It might be Lisa's day, but he was done explaining himself and reassuring her.

Conor captured Laura's fingers, curved his hand around her waist and turned her into his arms. "I was just asking your little sister to." He managed a wink for Lisa as he whisked her bridesmaid onto the dance floor in a swirl of candy-pink tulle. "When they get to the hokey pokey, I'm your man."

It took a few steps for him to find the rhythm of the music after the abrupt start. Laura seemed to struggle for a moment, too. She stumbled over his feet, her free hand brushing against his arm, tapping the middle of his chest, then grasping his arm again, as if she wasn't sure where to rest it. Conor caught the wayward hand and placed it on his shoulder. He tightened his hold behind her waist and pulled her hips into his so that they could match their steps without him crushing any of her toes with his big feet.

Leading her into the heart of the dancers, he dipped his mouth beside Laura's ear. "Thanks for the save."

"Anytime. But seriously?" She whacked his shoulder in a playful reprimand. "The hokey pokey? Avoiding my sister much?"

"A slow dance leaves too much time for talking. I've said my piece to Lisa."

"But you're okay to talk with me?"

"Yeah. I'm okay with that." That wasn't a lie. Something inside him eased a little bit. "If you can stand to talk to me after that whole Scott Swearingen fiasco."

"I know it's your go-to, but you don't have to make everything a joke. Not with me."

The music created a low, pulsing rhythm in Conor's blood. Or maybe that was simply the thumping of his heart after that close call with

Lisa. And maybe it had nothing to do with any woman other than the one he held in his arms. Laura stared right at the knot of his tie as they swayed together. But she did this crazy-cute thing when she spoke, tilting her eyes up to him. With his hand flattened at the small of her back, it wouldn't take much to tug her body flush against his. And for a few seconds, his fingers tightened against the ticklish lace, wanting to do just that.

Good grief. Had he not been with a woman since Lisa returned his ring? He mentally ran through his social calendar, or lack thereof, for the past two years. Hell. Had he even gone out on a date?

No wonder the enticing scent of Laura's hair was filling his head with non-brotherly thoughts. Just entertaining the idea of moving his hand to the curve of her rump or nuzzling his lips against the shell of her exposed ear shocked him into taking half a step back and thinking analytically about Laura. She had more curves to hold on to than Lisa ever had. Laura clearly took after her mother's side of the family, while Lisa favored their father. The crown of Laura's dark hair had touches of gold in it that Lisa's sable tresses lacked. The caramel highlights tipping each wave made Laura's hair color as uniquely unpredictable as the green and gold of her eyes.

"Have I ever danced with you before, Squirt—"

said green-gold eyes tilted his way and he caught himself "—Laura?"

"No. It's not as awkward as I imagined it would be." A rosy hue warmed her cheeks, and he wondered if he'd ever seen her blush before. "Because of the differences in our heights."

Wait. Why was she was blushing? "You imagined dancing with me?"

"Ego much, Detective?"

Conor laughed. "My ego's taken a few hard hits lately. It appreciates even the remnants of a teenage crush."

She glanced to the side and stiffened in his arms for a moment. Conor was about to ask if he'd offended her, when she hooked her hand behind his neck, moving in close enough for her breasts to brush against him. For a few seconds, as every sensible cell in his body rushed to those points of contact, he didn't even hear her words. "Lisa's glaring at us. She knows you're avoiding her. Are you okay with that? Or are we trying to make her mad?"

After inhaling a steadying breath, Conor eased a little space between them, ostensibly so he could look down into her eyes, but mostly because his body was firing in ways he wasn't entirely comfortable with around Laura. And he certainly didn't want her to realize the purely male interest in her that was stirring behind his zipper. "I'm not the retribution type. I'm okay with this marriage. But I don't have to be a glutton for punishment. I'm afraid getting too close will stir up things I'm not allowed to feel anymore."

Or shouldn't feel in the first place—like whatever was happening to him with Laura tonight.

"Lisa loved you, you know." She shrugged, as if apologizing for what she said next. "I just don't think she was *in* love with you."

Well, wasn't that a painfully sharp distinction to make? Time to change the subject to anything but him. "Did you ever get a date with that track star?"

"Nope. Decided he wasn't my type." Thankfully, Laura shifted the conversation with him. "That was almost a decade ago. I'm not a kid anymore. You just haven't been around to notice. I've earned a college degree. I have a career as an educational travel coordinator. I book and lead student tours. I've seen a lot of the country. A lot of the world."

"And I thought you wanted to grow up and play professional softball. Or be a veterinarian at a zoo—you wanted to save cheetahs or something like that. Or become a US marshal like your favorite neighbor."

Laura pulled her hand from his shoulder, laughing as she gestured to the generous swells of her breasts. "These got in the way of being an athlete. Allergy to cats precluded the vet job. And I outgrew my teenage crush on all things Conor Wildman long ago."

Conor covered his heart, laughing with her. "I'm wounded."

She teasingly punched his arm before grabbing his hand and pulling him back into the rhythm of the music. "All the years I would have traded anything for you to see me as more than your kid sister. Oh, well. You had your chance, big guy. I've moved on."

That particular choice of words sounded a little too familiar. Moving on was exactly what Lisa had done. Years ago, it was what his father had done, too.

Conor needed to save the conversation before he took a trip too far down the path of bitter memories. "I appreciate the flowers and letter you sent for Mom. That was sweet of you to recall some of the fun things we did growing up. Those were good memories. Mom treasured them as much as I did."

"They were. I'm so sorry about Marie." Laura stopped in the middle of the dance floor to slide her arms beneath his jacket and hug him around the waist.

Conor braced his feet, absorbing a bump from the couple moving next to them. When that accidental nudge didn't loosen her hold on him, he wound his arms around her shoulders, protecting her from the people moving around them. And, if he was honest with himself, relaxing into the curves of her body and the heat of her small form clinging to him, accepting the solace of the compassionate gesture. "You okay, Squirt?"

He felt the hum of her groan vibrating through the cotton of his shirt.

"Sorry." He dropped a kiss to the crown of her hair. "Laura. You okay?"

Her squeeze around him tightened. "I'm sorry I couldn't get back for the service. But I did go by the cemetery once I was in town. The marker wasn't up yet, but I left flowers at the site."

"Thank you." That reminded him that he needed to go by the cemetery and check the status of the headstone he'd ordered.

They were still hugging as the song ended. The DJ was encouraging the married couples in attendance to make their way to the dance floor for a competition to see who'd been together the longest. "That leaves us out." Conor finally relented his hold on Laura. She pulled away but latched onto his hand as he walked her back to the tables. "It really is good to see you, Laura."

"You, too, Conor. I've missed you."

"I appreciate a few minutes of normal amidst all the crazy." He chucked her lightly beneath the chin and grinned. "I don't have to pretend to smile with you."

When he excused himself to leave, she tugged on his tie with one hand and slipped the other around his neck, pulling him down for a kiss. What the heck? Her lips were warm, bowed and moving across his before he could close the startled O of his mouth. When he did press his lips together, they caught the decadent fullness of her lower lip between his. Whoa. Did that qualify as a kiss? Had he just kissed Laura? With a noise that sounded suspiciously like a moan beneath the pulse of the music, she pushed up onto her tiptoes, sealing their mouths together in another kiss that exploded somewhere inside his brain and lit a fuse down to his groin, prompting the instinctive need to snap her to his body and take over the embrace. But before he could even acknowledge the desire zinging through him, she dropped back onto her heels and broke the connection between them.

As he leaned over her like this, with her face tilted to his, the color of her eyes changed like a kaleidoscope, showing him tawny sparkles of glitter amidst the forest, moss and olive in her irises. The woman had beautiful eyes. "You should do that more," she whispered.

"Kiss?" He'd been too startled to respond the way he'd wanted to, but now he was wondering if he had... He could still feel the pressure of her lips softening against his...

She rubbed her fingertips across his mouth, probably wiping off a stray glob of lipstick. But he felt the tug of that unexpected touch down deep inside him. "Smile. You've always been such a good-looking son of a gun when you smile."

Was she flirting with him? How was he supposed to think brotherly thoughts when every cell of his body was standing at attention, eagerly anticipating the next touch? When every self-respecting male hormone was demanding he take her in his arms and show her that Conor Wildman knew exactly how to respond to a woman's kiss, and not stand there like a statue.

She smoothed his tie against his chest and stepped back, maybe sensing that he'd change the way that kiss had ended if she didn't put some space between them. "I'd better go. Try to get a hold of Chloe again."

Right. Get a grip, Wildman. That was a goodbye kiss. Hadn't he just been thanking her for keeping everything normal between them? *He* was the one putting a sensual spin on things.

A nod of agreement was the best he could do right now. "Good luck."

Conor watched her chat her way through the crowd before she disappeared into the same hallway where Isaac Royal had gone. These few minutes with Laura—their dance, that kiss—had been both the most natural and the most unsettling conversation he'd had all evening.

After enduring a couple of quick dances with Lisa, reassuring her every way he knew how that her marrying Joe hadn't damaged him beyond repair, he finally made his exit. He'd done his time. He'd saved face, rallied a bit of his pride. But he was more than ready to loosen his tie and unbutton the collar of his shirt as he pushed open the door to a rush of damp February air and strode across the parking lot to his SUV.

Conor inhaled deep breaths of the cold, sobering air into his lungs, replaying this whole evening, replaying the last two years, actually, calculating just how quickly he could wrap up his mother's business and get on the road to Kansas City before he got any more lost in the twilight zone of his old life.

He was halfway to his SUV and mentally halfway home to KC when Laura came running out of the shadows from between two cars and slammed into him.

"Whoa." He caught her by the shoulders and steadied her in front of him to keep her from falling. "Where's the fire?" Her bare arms were already dotted with goose bumps beneath his hands. His tone grew serious. "Where's your coat?"

She glanced back at the reception hall and muttered a choice word. "I'll get it later." A cloud of warm breath obscured her face for a moment before she broke away and hurried down the line of vehicles. "Chloe's in trouble."

"Your friend?" Conor fell into step beside her.

"I have to help her. I knew she was in over her head with Vinnie. It was just a stupid, stupid plan." She stopped beside a compact toaster of a car and sorted through the keys dangling from her fingers. Before she found the remote, she dropped her keys into the snow beneath the car. Laura dropped down in a billow of cotton-candy pink to search for them. Conor knelt to retrieve them for her. Not only had she run outside without a proper winter coat, but the only things she'd brought with her were the keys and the phone she clutched in her left hand. Where was her purse? Her driver's license?

Conor's fingers closed around the keys first and he stood. "You seem pretty upset, Squirt—"

"Stop calling me that. I'm a grown woman." She snatched the keys from his hand and tried to unlock her car. She tapped the remote a half dozen times. "Why isn't this working? Dad said to get the stupid battery replaced."

Conor brushed his fingers along her arm, trying to calm her. "Hey, I'm not the enemy here. Tell me what's wrong."

"Chloe had a fight with her boyfriend."

"You mean her fight with Isaac?"

"Vincent. The one she dumped Isaac for." She glanced a quick 360 around the parking lot. "Isaac's car isn't here. Maybe she called him, too. Why would she call me if she'd already talked to him? I don't know… She sounded wrong. She wasn't making sense. I have to get to her. I have a bad vibe about this."

"How bad a vibe?"

"Bad. She said she needs my help." Giving up on the remote, she pulled up a key to unlock the car the old-fashioned way.

Conor curled his hand around hers, stopping her from turning the key. "I don't know if you're in the right frame of mind to drive. Have you been drinking?"

"No!"

"Okay, okay. This just isn't you. At least, the you I remember. You're wiggin' out a little bit." She rolled her eyes up at him. *That* was a condemning look. *Fine. You're not a little girl anymore. I get that.* "You're that worried about her?"

"Yes. On the phone, when she finally called me back—she was out of breath. Like she'd been running or crying. Or she was hiding. Or hurt? She whispered everything. I kept asking her to repeat things."

"Why would she be hiding?"

She hugged her arms around her waist, shivering. From nerves? Cold? A combination of both? "I'm not sure. I don't think she was alone, and she didn't want whoever was there to overhear. I could hear a man talking, but I couldn't make out any words. Music was playing. She had it up loud."

"What exactly did she say?"

"She said she was eloping with Vinnie—that she talked him into proposing to her. They're driving to the airport. And then there was something about insurance and she's counting on me to keep it safe and her mom could never find out, and she was hoping she wouldn't have to use it."

"Keep what safe?"

"I don't know. She thanked me and said I was her best friend and that she had to go."

"Go where?"

Laura turned the key in the lock. "Stop asking me questions like you're a cop and I'm a suspect."

"I *am* a cop." Her cheeks were pale, her whole body trembling when she glared at him a second time. Conor shrugged out of his suit jacket and draped it around her. Whether she was freezing or about to burst into tears didn't matter. He clasped her shoulders and rubbed his hands up and down her arms, instilling what warmth and support he could through the jacket. "You're upset. Enough that you're scaring me a little bit. Talk to me."

The glare was gone when she tilted her gaze to his. "Vegas. She said they're going to Las Vegas. They'll get the rings and everything they need there."

"They're not the first couple to do that. You said Chloe was impulsive. Sounds like they both are. Are you worried she'll have regrets?"

"She asked me to feed her cat."

And that was a problem because...? "Do you have a key to her apartment? Will the landlord let you in?" Then he remembered something she'd mentioned on the dance floor. "Are you worried about your allergies?"

"She doesn't have a cat!" She shrugged off his touch and opened the car door.

Conor palmed the window and closed it again. Either that remark about the cat had been a coded plea for help, or they were the words of someone who wasn't in her right mind enough to make a big decision like elopement. Laura knew that, too.

Now he understood her panic, her need to act.

There was little Conor could explain about the ups and downs of all that had happened this evening. But he knew how to answer a call for help.

"I'll drive." He captured Laura by the elbow and walked her to his car, bundling her into the passenger seat before starting the engine and cranking up the heat. "Keep calling your friend. And tell me everything you know about Chloe and Vincent Orlando."

Chapter Three

Living out your teenage fantasy much?

Laura's hands were shaking as she dug through the contents of her kitchen junk drawer to find the smiley-faced key chain Chloe had given her. Conor lurked in the living room of her one-bedroom apartment, scoping out her eclectic décor filled with antiques and travel souvenirs. Or maybe he was keeping his distance while he wondered what was wrong with her.

What on earth had possessed her to kiss him like that? No friendly peck on the lips, no polite buss across the cheek—but a full-on, hey-I-have-the-hots-for-you kind of kiss. The kind of kiss that left a smear of lipstick and stamp of wishful possession on his mouth for all to see.

Conor had no reason to stay in Arlington. No reason to give her a chance to prove that her feelings for him had matured as much as she had.

He was leaving. Going back to Kansas City.

Leaving her behind without ever knowing how she really felt about him. Again.

Laura closed her eyes and breathed in the spicy smell of him that lingered on his jacket. He'd pulled a long wool coat from the back of his SUV to put on while she slid her arms inside his suit jacket and rolled up the sleeves. The warmth from his body she'd felt when he'd put it on her was long gone, yet the sensations of being sheltered and cherished remained.

But it was all an illusion of intimacy. Polite concern for her well-being was about as romantic as he ever intended to get with her. That rescue dance at the reception had awakened all the old feelings inside her that had never truly died. Not through growing up and taking separate paths. Not through grief. Not through seeing him give his heart to the wrong sister and being gutted by her rejection. Not through her inability to let any man claim her own heart the way Conor unknowingly had.

She knew the sound of his goodbyes. So, she'd kissed him. Because the chance to pretend Conor Wildman could be hers for even a few moments before he walked away, before she ever had the chance to show him how she felt, was just too great to resist.

But he hadn't kissed her back.

In terms of emotional self-preservation, it

wasn't the smartest move she'd ever made. Clearly, Conor still thought of her as fifteen and in need of a big brother, instead of twenty-five and ready to go after the man she wanted—even risking their lifelong friendship to do so—so the kiss was probably just a whole weird, uncomfortable thing for him.

She should be content with friend status because, after Chloe's cryptic phone call and Isaac's can't-be-bothered-with-her attitude, she needed a good friend right about now. Something was wrong, judging by that call. It was a cry for help she didn't understand, but Laura had no intention of ignoring it.

Affirming that her priorities were in their proper place, she fisted the key to Chloe's apartment in her hand and hurried past Conor out the door.

By the time they reached the stairs beside the elevator, Laura had pushed aside all fantasies of kissing Conor, reluctantly accepting that he would never see her as anything more than Lisa's kid sister. With the tall, lanky frustration following her every step of the way, she hurried up the stairs and down the hallway to the apartment above hers.

She was glad Conor had driven, not because she didn't think she could squash the panic enough to get herself safely home, but because she wanted someone with her for moral support. Laura's worries about Chloe were all over the board, leaving her thoughts scattered and her heart racing. Until she had some answers, she was imagining all kinds of worst-case scenarios that her friend might have gotten herself into—having her heart broken by Vinnie, getting stranded in Vegas. Her comment about wanting Laura to guard an insurance policy was still a puzzle. She knew darn well that Chloe barely kept up the payments on her car and renter's insurance, and that was only done with Isaac managing things for her. The kind of insurance Chloe had talked about sounded a little bit like blackmail. Laura didn't have to be a criminologist to know that the person being blackmailed tended not to like being coerced into doing something against his or her will. Maybe Vinnie had done something worse than break her friend's heart. Maybe he'd talked Chloe into doing something dangerous or illegal for him. Maybe the marriage offer had been the bargaining chip he'd used to get Chloe to help him.

Chloe might be a free spirit who danced to her own tune, but she'd never once done anything so bizarre as give Laura a message about her non-existent cat. Unless she'd impulsively gone out and adopted herself one, in which case, Laura's temper would boil over for all the unnecessary stress she'd caused her today. While she stewed and speculated, Conor was in clearheaded cop mode, with no emotional ties to Chloe to cloud his thinking.

Conor was here as her friend. Laura was grateful, humiliated and heartbroken all at the same time.

Damn. She never should have kissed him.

"Here it is." Reaching apartment C-8, she knocked on the door and waited. "We water plants and pick up each other's mail when we travel." She knocked on the door again before sliding the key into the lock and twisting the dead bolt. "Chloe? You here? It's Laura. I'm coming in."

She pushed open the door, flipped on the light switch and froze.

In the split second it took for Laura to take in the utter devastation of Chloe's ransacked apartment, Conor had grasped her shoulders and pulled her back into the open doorway.

He moved between Laura and the shredded sofa cushions, broken picture frames, shattered knick-knacks and pages from her precious art books torn and tossed across the floor. "Miss Wilson? I'm Detective Wildman," he announced. "A friend of Laura's. Are you here? Are you all right?" He pulled back the front of his jacket and patted his belt.

Laura's blood ran even colder when he pulled his hand away with a muttered curse. He was looking for his gun. He thought whatever had happened here was really, *really* bad. She stiffened at the tension radiating off him. She'd been right to worry. "Conor?"

He pulled his badge from his pocket and clipped it to his belt before reaching back to squeeze her shoulder. "Stay here. Call 9-1-1. Report a break-in."

"You think this is a robbery? It looks so...violent." She scanned the main room from one wall to the other. No piece of furniture was untouched by the chaos. "Chloe?"

"Call." Conor's long, smooth strides, quickly taking him from room to room with a sharply uttered "Clear," made her think he believed this was something more, too. *Clear* meant there was no sign of Chloe, right?

But was that a good thing or a bad thing?

Tamping down the urge to shake in her sparkly heels, Laura pulled out her cell and dialed the police. "My neighbor asked me to come over and check on her place," she explained to the dispatcher. "Someone has completely trashed her apartment." Her eyes never left Conor while she gave the address and answered questions. She noted the details as best she could. Plants had been dumped from their pots on the windowsill, the dirt strewn across the hardwood floor beside Chloe's desk. "Her computer is missing." The dispatcher probably didn't care about the colorful ceramic statuary that had been knocked to the carpet or broken against a harder surface, or the hand-sewn pillows that had been cut open and had their stuffing pulled out. Laura frowned. "Her television is still here. To be honest, it looks as though there was a terrible fight, or the intruder was looking for something." But what that might be she couldn't tell the dispatcher. "No, she doesn't keep a lot of money here. She doesn't have a lot of money." Almost anything of value here, besides her artwork, had been given to Chloe by one of her boyfriends. When the dispatcher asked about precious jewelry, Laura moved toward the bedroom, clinging close to the wall—partly so she wouldn't disturb anything, but mostly because there was no other safe way to move through the main room. "She inherited some gold beads from her grandmother when she passed away. Yes, I'm checking for the necklace now."

Conor met her at the closed door to Chloe's bedroom, looking none too pleased that she hadn't remained near the hallway. "I told you to wait—"

"Scowl away, Wildman. The dispatcher wants me to—"

"Let me." He held up a white handkerchief in

his hand that he used to turn the doorknob. "The police will want to dust for fingerprints, and I don't want them to find yours."

She nodded, appreciating his caution, before turning her attention back to the woman on the other end of the call. "The jewelry box is…"

Laura screamed.

Conor swore and turned her away from the gruesome sight.

He plucked the cell phone from her fingers and rattled off some official-sounding words like "badge number" and "bus" and "home invasion." Clutching at his shirt and jacket as he backed them both out of the room, Laura buried her face in his chest.

But she couldn't bury the image of Chloe Wilson's bruised body trapped beneath the drawers of her overturned dresser, her skull bashed in and her blond hair floating in a pool of blood.

Chapter Four

"And now for Miss Prom Night." Deputy T. J. Cobb turned away from the body bag on a gurney the medical examiner was wheeling down the hallway and pointed to Laura. He ordered another deputy to give them some privacy and gestured to the unoccupied apartment across the hall where he'd been conducting interviews. Once she'd entered the empty beige space, Deputy Cobb pulled a small notepad from inside his jacket and tapped it with his finger. "You and I need to talk, little lady."

"Don't patronize me, sir." Laura had changed into her suede and sheepskin boots and returned to join the gathering of neighbors, crime scene techs and uniformed deputies gathered outside the yellow tape stuck across the door to Chloe's apartment. She wished now that she hadn't listened to Conor's suggestion that she go downstairs to her apartment to regroup a bit while he waited for the local authorities to arrive and take his statement. She didn't care that she looked like a little girl playing dress-up in her poufy bridesmaid's dress, Conor's suit jacket and her winter boots. But she did care that the flat boots made her the shortest adult here, save for her mom, who was waiting with her dad down in her place, in case she needed their support. She had a feeling she would, especially if the deputy couldn't see beyond her girlish looks and speak to her as an adult. "I am perfectly capable of answering any questions you have."

"Fair enough." The way Deputy Cobb smiled down at her around the toothpick wedged between his teeth made Laura feel like he was a starving man and she was the last morsel left on one of the canapé trays at Lisa's wedding reception. Nor was she comforted by his dubious good ol' boy charm. "How come you're all dolled up?" he asked.

Laura curled her fingers into the wool of Conor's jacket, clutching the lapels together at the base of her throat. She hadn't felt warm since she and Conor had discovered her friend's body, but she guessed the sea of goose bumps dotting her arms now had more to do with shock than with the wintry temperature outside. "I was at my sister's wedding. Shouldn't you be asking me about Chloe? Miss Wilson?" She heard the ding of the elevator arriving on the third floor, thought of her friend's half-dressed body being hauled away in a bag like discarded trash, and shivered. "The victim?"

"We'll get there." He shoved his flat-brimmed hat back on his head and scratched at his curly blond hair before glancing down at his notepad. "It's Laura Karr with a K, isn't it? You live downstairs?"

Laura nodded. "Apartment B-8." She hated how long it took Deputy Cobb to complete a sentence, as if he had all the time in the world to bring Chloe's killer to justice. As if finding out the truth wasn't as urgent a priority for him as it was for her.

"Well, Ms. Karr with a K... You always a nosy neighbor?" The deputy's tongue darted between his teeth to move his toothpick from one side of his mouth to the other. "You messed up my crime scene."

Was that an accusation? His lazy-drawled attempt to upset her enough to reveal something he thought she knew? She bit down on the frustration that wanted to spew out and kept her voice as even as she could manage. "I was worried about my friend. She called me."

"Called you? We didn't find any cell phone in there. No landline."

"I don't know anything about that. She called me earlier. At the wedding reception. She was in trouble. As soon as I opened the door…" She shook her head to dispel the memory of all the destruction. "I didn't touch anything."

"The bedroom is at the back of the apartment. You're saying you didn't walk through that apartment to get to your friend?"

"You saw what it looked like. I was concerned for Chloe's safety. Rightly so."

The flurry of voices in the hallway behind her barely registered.

He pulled the toothpick from between his lips and pointed it at her. "Did you and your friend have a falling out?"

"No."

"Traipsing through Miss Wilson's apartment was either a careless act on your part, or you were intentionally trying to sabotage any clues that might tell us what happened to your friend."

Laura bristled at his thinly veiled allegation. "I didn't sabotage anything."

"We can't even tell if that lock was forced."

"It wasn't." A familiar, deep voice clipped through the air behind her. Conor. Relief huffed out in an audible sigh. When the man at the door tried to stop him, Conor pointed to the badge prominently displayed on the chest pocket of his coat—right next to the spot where the officer was restraining him. "Detective Wildman. And you're going to lose that hand if you don't let me in to see Miss Karr."

Cobb looked from her up to Conor, then shrugged and stuffed the toothpick back between his lips. "Let him in."

Laura felt Conor's hand at the small of her back before he spoke again. "She can't tell you anything about the crime scene I haven't already told you. We used a spare key the victim gave her to get in. As an officer of the law, I entered the premises because we feared for Miss Wilson's safety. I know crime scene protocol. We touched nothing. As soon as we found the body, we went back out into the hall and waited for you and your men to arrive."

Not only could she feel Conor's warmth radiating against her side like an infusion of life-giving sustenance, she could feel the gun and holster he'd strapped onto his belt. He must have gone out to his SUV and suited up into full cop mode while she'd been putting on her silly, cushy boots. She hadn't handled anything very well tonight—not her concern for Chloe, not that impulsive kiss and certainly not her friend's murder. No wonder Conor still looked at her like the kid next door, and not a mature woman.

She needed to do something, say something, be something more than a woman who was too upset or intimidated to stand up for herself. She appreciated Conor's staunch support, but she needed to summon her own strength. She tilted her chin to meet the deputy's pale green eyes. "There was no blood anywhere else in that apartment. The murder occurred in that bedroom, and we never went in there." She glanced up at Conor. "Detective Wildman got us both out of there as soon as we discovered the body."

Conor nodded. "The rest of the damage happened separately from the struggle in Miss Wilson's bedroom. Someone was looking for something—either she surprised the intruder who expected her to be gone, or the search happened after she was killed."

The deputy rolled his toothpick between his teeth and laughed. "And I'm just supposed to take your word for that?"

"Yes."

Deputy Cobb tucked his notebook back inside his jacket without writing anything down. "I don't know you, Wildman. You're not a cop from around here, so I don't have to take your word on anything." He flicked his gaze down to Laura. "And you ain't no kind of cop at all."

"I know what I saw," Laura argued.

Conor rubbed his hand up and down her spine through the jacket she wore, as if he could feel some of that backbone she was growing again.

"Read your manual. Observations like that are basic police work."

Cobb didn't seem too pleased with the reminder. "You said you were a US marshal when you lived in Arlington. You're in witness protection, not homicide investigation."

"That was my old life. I'm an investigator with KCPD now."

"Still ain't your case. I can book you for interfering with my investigation."

"And I can file charges against you for professional misconduct and witness intimidation." Cobb chuckled, as if he liked, or at least respected, Conor's refusal to back down. Conor didn't seem to care about Cobb's opinion, one way or the other. "Do you have anything further to ask Miss Karr?"

"I'm done for now." The deputy straightened the brim of his hat. "But don't you go leaving town. I might call you in for more questions. Both of you." He took a couple of steps toward the door before glancing back. "You sure you didn't touch or remove anything from that apartment?"

The defensive *no* on Laura's lips was drowned out by a man's frantic voice booming through the hallway.

"That's Chloe's place. What happened? Is that…?" She recognized the despair, even if she couldn't immediately identify the speaker. "Oh, my God. Chloe!"

Deputy Cobb barked a curse word. "What now?" He pushed past the other deputy into the hallway before giving the younger officer a command. "Get these people out of here." Laura recognized the dark ponytail and sharply defined cheekbones of Chloe's latest boyfriend. Cobb palmed him in the middle of the chest and stopped him in his tracks as he tried to duck beneath the crime scene tape into Chloe's apartment. "Hold up a minute there. Who are you?"

"Vinnie Orlando. I need to see Chloe."

"You the boyfriend?" Cobb asked.

Vinnie looked dazed as he nodded to the barrel-chested deputy and took note of Laura, Conor and the retreating lookie-loos being ushered into their respective apartments. He spun back to the closing elevator doors where two of Vinnie's buddies waited with their hands stuck inside the pockets of their winter coats. A fourth man with salt-and-pepper hair, wearing a tailored wool dress coat and expensive leather gloves, strode up behind Vinnie. Vinnie took a few steps toward the older man before swinging back to face the deputy. "Yeah, I... The body that guy was pushing onto the elevator—was that her? Is Chloe really...?" His face flushed the color of dark bricks as he tried to get a grip on his emotions. "She was supposed to wait… We were gonna meet…" The older man clasped his shoulder in a gesture of comfort. "Where is he taking her? Can I see her?"

Laura stepped forward, feeling his grief twisting in her own gut. She reached for Vinnie's gloved hand and squeezed it between both of hers. "I don't know if you remember me, Vinnie. But we've met. I'm so sorry for your loss. I know Chloe really cared about you. But you don't want to see her like this. Just think about how beautiful she was—how much she loved to laugh and smile."

"Thanks." He nodded, squeezing her hand before releasing her. "Loni, right?"

She stepped back to Conor's side. Although her heart went out to his grief, her bad vibe about the self-centered twentysomething hadn't changed. "Laura. I was Chloe's friend."

He shrugged off the older man's comfort and swiped his hand over his cheeks and jaw, probably staving off the urge to burst into tears. "Sure. I remember you. You were at that bar with Chloe and me that one night."

"I never went bar-hopping with you two. We met here in Chloe's apartment. I was helping her paint her bedroom. You stopped by and told her to clean up for an impromptu road trip. You'd just gotten a convertible."

Vinnie frowned, clearly not remembering the introduction. "Did she come with me?"

"Oh, yes. She had lots of great things to say about that day. I stayed behind and finished the paint job."

"Yeah, that was a sweet car." Laura didn't take offense at being too insignificant for him to remember. Not tonight. Not with losing the woman he loved—or at least cared about. That is, she didn't take offense until he asked the next question. "You saw her tonight? Was Chloe wearing a ring? Did the guy who broke into her apartment steal the ring I gave her? It was my mother's."

Deputy Cobb pulled out his notepad again. "A ring?"

"You're worried about a theft? Chloe's dead. You understand that, right?" Not her finest moment of compassion, but there seemed to be a whole lot of not caring about what had happened to her friend going around.

The older man reached inside the front of his coat. "It's an engagement ring. Vincent and Miss Wilson were close."

Laura frowned. "She told me you were getting the rings in Las Vegas."

Vinnie sputtered, as if surprised to be contradicted. "She told you we were getting married?"

"She called me earlier this evening. Said getting married was a guarantee. But she never mentioned you already giving her a ring."

"Oh." That seemed to be news to him. Was Vinnie surprised that Chloe had shared the news of their elopement, or surprised to be getting married, period? "Yeah. Right."

The older man pulled out his wallet and extracted a business card. "Deputy, we need to find that ring. May we go inside and look for it?"

Laura replayed that last weird conversation she'd had with Chloe in her head, then fast-forwarded to entering the apartment less than two hours ago. Had Chloe been wearing an engagement ring? Laura hadn't looked. She hadn't seen anything beyond the blood and Chloe's dim, sightless eyes.

"It's a family heirloom," the older man explained, his tone coolly articulate in contrast to Vinnie's manic roller coaster of emotions. "A priceless family heirloom Mr. Orlando would like to get back."

"And you are?" Cobb asked.

"Marvin Boltz." He handed his card to the deputy. "I'm Mr. Orlando's attorney."

"You brought your attorney with you to see if your girlfriend was okay?"

Vinnie shook his head, taking a step toward the ransacked apartment before Cobb blocked his path. "No. Marv was already with me. He had a legal thing I had to sign—"

The man with the salt-and-pepper hair pulled Vinnie back to his side. "Don't say another word, Vincent."

"He damn well better keep talkin'." At last, T. J. Cobb seemed to be asking the right questions to the right person. "Were you here earlier? Did you tear up her apartment looking for that ring?"

Vinnie glanced at his attorney before answering. "I want to help. It's Chloe we're talking about. No. I didn't look for the ring."

Was that a lie? A version of the truth? Could he have torn up the apartment looking for something else? Like *insurance*? Or was there something special about that ring, like it was stolen property, or borrowed from his mother without consent, and he needed to get it back? Was that reason enough to commit murder?

She'd almost forgotten Conor hadn't left when his shadow loomed up beside her. He pushed Vinnie for more details. "When was the last time you saw Miss Wilson? The last time you talked to her?"

"Why are you still here, Detective?" Cobb snarled. "This is my investigation." He turned back to Vinnie. "But I'd be interested in your answers."

Marvin Boltz shook his head and turned away

from the conversation while Vinnie answered. "Yesterday evening. I was here with her all yesterday afternoon. We were, you know, intimate. She was into me. She was hot."

That explained why Chloe hadn't come to the wedding. Maybe being so *into* Vinnie even explained why she hadn't answered any of Laura's calls or texts.

"So, you two shared some afternoon delight, and then you left," Cobb clarified.

"Yeah. I had to take care of some things. Business. Isn't that right, Marvin?"

The attorney shrugged, looking surprised to hear his client consult him. "That's right."

Laura couldn't help but wonder what kind of business Vinnie was in, and why he'd be conducting it late on a Saturday afternoon. Since he hadn't deigned to have any kind of get-acquainted conversation with her when they'd met, she asked, "Are you a lawyer, too?"

Vinnie laughed. "And stay in school that long? Hell no, Marvin's an old family friend. I'm…" Now his lawyer was glaring. "I'm an artist, like Chloe was."

A very successful one, judging by the designer cut of his leather coat, the well-tailored attorney and the beefy entourage who watched from the elevator doors. "You're a sculptor?"

"Painter," he answered, flicking his ponytail

from the collar of his jacket. "I painted Chloe a few times."

The deputy held up his hand, dismissing what he probably considered to be chitchat. "How was she when you left? Were you planning on seeing her again?"

"She was verrrry satisfied when I left." He laughed at his own joke, then shrugged when he realized nobody else in the hallway was laughing. "I was supposed to meet her tomorrow morning. *This* morning, I guess. We're going to Vegas to get married. *Were* going. Hell. She's really gone?"

The stairwell door swung open behind Laura, and Isaac Royal tottered out. "You know she is, you son of a bitch!"

Laura startled at Isaac's sudden entrance, and her fingers accidentally brushed against Conor's down at her side. For the briefest of moments, he laced his fingers through hers and clasped her hand. But instead of offering comfort, he was nudging her out of harm's way as Isaac charged at Vinnie.

His slurred speech and stumbling balance didn't stop him from barreling into the larger, more muscular man. "What did you do to my Chloe?"

Vinnie's two buddies rushed down the hallway, grabbing Isaac by the arms after the first shove.

Vinnie pushed back, knocking Isaac's glasses to the floor. "Out of my face, loser," he taunted.

"You son of a bitch. I loved her!"

"She was mine."

Isaac's hand fisted as if he wanted to throw a punch, but one of the bruisers caught him by the wrist and twisted it up behind his back as he rammed him into the wall. Conor pushed Vinnie against the opposite wall, holding him in place while Deputy Cobb moved between the brawling men.

The deputy leaned closer to Isaac's ear. "What's your name, son?"

"Isaac Royal," he spat. Laura realized she wasn't the only one still wearing wedding garb. Only hers was in better condition than the stained shirt cuff and torn sleeve of Isaac's tuxedo.

She also realized that the fist pinned in the middle of Isaac's back was bruised and swollen around several small, fresh cuts. "Isaac, are you okay?"

"Chloe's dead," he yelled, before his voice hushed with a quiet sob. "How can I be okay?"

"Let him go, Rico." At a nod from Marvin Boltz, the two men who seemed to be more bodyguards than buddies released Isaac. Conor let go of Vinnie and backed away while Isaac rubbed at his twisted arm, whimpering with unabashed grief or pain.

Marvin took hold of his client's arm and pulled him aside, warning his buddies to get Vinnie on the elevator while he wrapped things up. "If there's nothing else, Mr. Cobb?"

"Not right now. I've got your contact information."

With those men dismissed, Cobb turned his attention to Isaac. "You safe to be driving, son?"

Isaac nodded. "I took a cab."

"Good. Take one home and sleep it off." Then the deputy turned away and ducked beneath the crime scene tape.

Conor stopped Cobb before he got beyond the doorway. "You're not going to interview Royal?"

"Not in the state he's in. Unreliable witness." He tipped the brim of his hat to Laura, dismissing them, too. "You folks better get on home."

Laura opened her mouth to protest the deputy's mercurial investigative skills, but Conor shook his head, nodding toward the empty room across the hall. Good. This might not be his case, or even his jurisdiction, but Conor wasn't going to let her down. She needed answers, and whether he was doing his job, or he was being a good friend, he was going to help her find out what had happened to Chloe. Nodding her understanding, Laura scooped up Isaac's glasses and linked her arm through his, leading the distraught man into the empty apartment.

Conor followed them inside and pulled the door to. Isaac leaned back against the wall, tears dripping from his jaw onto the lapel of his tux before putting on the glasses Laura handed him.

She pulled out the tissue her mother had insisted she tuck inside the bodice of her dress before the wedding and handed it to Isaac. "I'm so sorry." She would have stepped in to give him a hug, but his tux smelled of smoke and alcohol, and she didn't think he was the hugging type, anyway. "I know your time with Chloe wasn't all picture-perfect, but I also know you loved her. And I know you want to find out what happened to her."

"What happened?" Isaac grumbled a derisive word under his breath. "It's Pretty Boy Vinnie out there who's responsible. He came into her life and ruined everything."

"Maybe." Conor's tone was surprisingly conversational, considering the gun and badge and strictly-business attitude he wore. "Where were you tonight?"

"At my friend's wedding. Just like you."

"Not the whole time. You left early."

Isaac shoved off the wall and headed for the door. "Get the hell away from me."

Laura caught him by the elbow, silently asking him to stay. "Isaac, please. You said that you and Chloe had a fight. When was that?"

"This afternoon… Yesterday afternoon, I guess."

She slid her hand a little farther down his sleeve and gently touched his wrist. "What happened to your hand?"

"I went to a bar after I left the reception. I tried to call Chloe, but she wouldn't answer. I was a little too angry. A little too drunk. I punched the mirror in the bathroom there." He held up his swollen, discolored hand, eyeing the cut that was still oozing on his middle finger. Then he quickly fisted the hand and dropped it to his side. "Wait. You think I did this?"

"She dumped you. And clearly you have a temper." Laura hesitated. "Her death was…violent."

"Oh, this is rich. I'm the only one mourning for her."

"That's not true." Laura tried to calm him down, but alcohol and anger kept him from listening.

"You think Orlando out there is grieving? He's probably just mad that her dying screwed up his weekend plans."

"What's the name of the bar where you were drinking?" Conor asked. "Can someone there verify when you arrived and when you left? Do they have a broken mirror to back up your story?"

"You got a lot of nerve, accusing me of anything." When Conor didn't budge out of his path,

Isaac directed his anger at Laura. "You and your boyfriend both."

"He's not my…" Laura started.

"I'm not her…" Conor echoed at the same time.

"Whatever. I've never been angry enough with Chloe to hurt her like that." His temper seemed to finally burn out and he leaned against the wall, sliding down to the floor until he could bury his face in his hands. "She was fine the last time I saw her. She was so happy—but it didn't have anything to do with me. She showed me some stupid white envelope—called it her insurance. She kissed it, left a big red lipstick mark on it— and said what was inside would make sure she got married this weekend. In case love wasn't enough."

Conor looked over Isaac's bowed head to Lisa. "I didn't see any lipstick-marked envelope. And there was other mail on the kitchen counter." He squatted down beside the bereaved man. "Did you see any kind of ring she was wearing?"

Isaac shook his head. "All I was seeing was red. She had the gall to ask me to drive to the post office to mail that package for her before the wedding."

"She was still planning on going to Lisa and Joe's wedding?" Laura asked. Afternoon delight with Vinnie might have ended a little sooner than the ponytailed hunk had indicated.

"I guess."

What kept her from going to the church? What changed? Who had stopped her from getting to the ceremony and reception?

"Who was she sending the envelope to?" Conor asked, pulling her from her speculation and moving the interrogation forward.

Isaac simply shook his head.

Laura knelt on the other side of Isaac and rested her hand on his shoulder. "Could there have been an insurance form in that envelope?" She hesitated, hating to think of the possible motive. "Like maybe someone took a policy out on her before he killed her? She said something about insurance to me, too."

"I don't know what was in the envelope. It wasn't a document envelope like my firm sends out. It was padded, lumpy."

"Could it have been a ring?" Laura speculated. Maybe Vinnie had already found what he'd been looking for, and his appearance tonight was all about throwing Deputy Cobb off his trail.

"She didn't show me, and I didn't ask. She wanted me to be happy for her—that she was finally going to have it all. I told her to go to hell, and I left." Isaac's tears started again. "'Go to hell.' Those were the last words I said to her."

Laura rubbed her hand up and down his arm. "You were hurting. Chloe knew you cared about her."

"I loved her," Isaac stated bluntly. "But it wasn't mutual. She needed me, but she didn't love me. I always thought if I was patient enough, that she'd give me a chance. But then Vinnie and his money came along…"

Conor stood, catching Isaac by the elbow and pulling him to his feet. "I need you to tell all this to Deputy Cobb."

"You need to be talking to Chloe's boy toy out there. The one she dumped me for." His dark eyes cleared their alcoholic haze for a moment, anger replacing his grief as he looked down at Laura. "I found Vinnie in her bed when I went to pick her up yesterday afternoon. That's why I said he could take her to the damn wedding."

Laura pulled her cell phone from the pocket of Conor's suit jacket. "Would you let me take a picture of your hand before you leave?" The fact that he didn't protest told her he was succumbing to his fatigue and emotions.

"Do you want me to drive you to the ER, so a doctor can look at those cuts?" Conor offered.

"To have them swab for DNA to prove whatever the hell you think I've done? No thanks." Isaac turned to Laura. "I used up my cash getting here. Will you float me a loan to get home?"

"I've got it covered," Conor offered, pulling out his wallet. When Isaac would have draped his arm around Laura's shoulders, Conor wound his arm behind the drunk man's waist and pulled him to his side to walk him out to the elevator himself. "For the record, any DNA the hospital pulled off you would be inadmissible in court, because I'm not in the chain of command on this case."

"You trying to be my friend now, Wildman?" Isaac slurred with contempt.

"Nope. I'm trying to be Laura's and get you to take care of yourself." Dark blue eyes met hers over the top of Isaac's head. "So that worry mark between her eyes will go away."

Chapter Five

"Thanks for helping get Isaac loaded into a cab." Laura carried Conor's mug to the sink and rinsed out the dregs of his coffee along with the rest of the pot her mother had made for them. "And thanks for convincing Mom and Dad it was okay to go home. It has been a super long day for them. Between the wedding and the murder, I know they're exhausted."

"But you're immune?"

She laughed, rinsing out the carafe and putting it back in the coffee maker. "All I want to do is fall into bed. And take off this gut-pinching corset and fluff of a dress."

He stood from the stool on the far side of the peninsula countertop and brought her the two plates on which they'd finally gotten to eat some leftover cake from the reception. Another gift from her mother. "I don't know." He batted at the fascinator still clipped to her hair. "I think *flamingo* is a good look on you."

She laughed with him, butting her shoulder against Conor's arm. He was warm and immovable and a better tonic for her glum 5:00 a.m. mood than sugar and caffeine had been. "Thanks. I was hoping it wasn't just me. 'Bridesmaid or Die' was my motto to get me through all the wedding planning and dress fittings. Can't tell you how many times I said that. No one else appreciated the joke."

"You came through the day with flying colors. The night, too." He checked his watch before rolling down the sleeves of his rumpled white shirt and buttoning the cuffs. "The sun will be up in another couple of hours. You gonna be okay?" He picked up his coat from the back of the stool and pulled it on. "You sure you don't want me to stay and keep an eye on things for a couple of hours while you take a nap or grab a shower or something?"

She quickly squashed her heart's eager response to his offer and waved aside the suggestion. She'd had Conor's full, protective attention through most of the night. She shouldn't be craving anything more. "I'll be okay. It's been a long twenty-four hours or so for you, too." She linked her arm through his and walked him to her front door. "I know you have stuff you wanted to get done today. Sorry to keep you up so late."

He stepped into the hallway but turned to her before leaving. "Not a problem, Squirt."

"What am I going to do with you, Wildman?" She crossed her arms and leaned against the doorframe, looking up into midnight blue eyes that were as familiar as the juvenile nickname. The golden scruff of his nearly twenty-four-hour beard growth dusting his cheeks and jaw was less familiar. His unbuttoned collar combined with his need for a shave felt intimate, as if they were evidence they'd shared the night together. In a way, they had. But certainly not in any way she'd fantasized about since she'd been old enough to think intimate thoughts about a man.

There were other details that were different tonight, too, details that twisted at her heartstrings. In the pocket of light from the hallway sconce beside her door, Conor's face was more guarded than she remembered, the laugh lines beside his eyes more pronounced with fatigue. He was all mystery and angles and mature man, and Laura's pulse fluttered in a purely female response.

But he wasn't here to stir her hormones or her heart. This wasn't the tender end to a special date. She was the only one imagining the intimacy of the two of them alone in the hallway, speaking in hushed tones as her neighbors slept. Laura mentally shook her head, warning her heart to be grateful for Conor's concern, and not ruing her inability to measure up to the love he had for her sister. "I just wish Cobb would have listened to what Isaac told us. At the very least he'd know that Vinnie might have been the last person to see Chloe alive yesterday."

But Cobb had shut down their efforts to report Isaac's account of his last argument with Chloe. "*Secondhand information is worse than no information at all,*" he'd said.

Laura filled her lungs with a deep breath that smelled like Conor and coffee and exhaled her despair at their hopes of finding Chloe's killer. "He's not a very good cop, is he."

"Not that I can see. But I'll stay on top of him as long as I'm here in town." Conor glanced down the hall to the elevator, as if he'd heard a sound, or sensed another presence. Maybe he was just anxious to leave now that the worst of the crisis had passed. "I still have a few connections here who can keep tabs on the investigation for me. For us."

"Thank you. I don't know what I would have done if you hadn't been here with me tonight."

His gaze locked on to hers again and he smiled. "You'd have handled it."

"I would have probably blown my stack at Cobb, or spent the night bawling my eyes out. Instead, you helped me do something about it. Even if we don't have answers yet. At least we tried."

Conor braced his hand on the doorframe above her head, his smile turning wry. "Beats trying to pretend I was the happiest guest at Lisa's wedding."

Right. Without the distraction of using his detective skills, he was probably thinking about how Lisa's decision to marry someone else had crushed him. Maybe it wasn't Laura specifically he wasn't romantically interested in—maybe Conor wasn't interested in loving *anyone*. If sarcasm was his go-to defense when dealing with the gruesome aspects of his work and the stresses of life, then complete avoidance of any entanglement might be how he protected his heart. She needed to accept that and be as good a friend to him as he'd been to her.

"I'm sure Lisa bought your act," she assured him. When she shrugged, her hair snagged in the nubby wool of Conor's jacket. She unbuttoned the front and took it off, feeling an instant chill as she lost its warmth and the care it symbolized. She folded it as neatly as she could before handing it to him. She'd already emptied her keys and phone out on the kitchen table. "Sorry about the wrinkles. I suppose we should both try to get a little sleep before sunrise."

"I don't mind staying," he offered, tossing the jacket over his shoulder. "Looks like your couch might hold most of me."

Laura smiled. Marie Wildman had raised her boy right. He was going to be chivalrous and protective even if it cost him a night's sleep and gave him a crick in the neck. "I'm fine. The police are done talking to me, right?"

"For now. If something else comes up, they might contact you again to double-check your information. But that won't happen until later."

"Then I'll be fine. I do want to get a few hours' sleep. I need to run by the reception hall and get my things and my car—Mom or Dad can drive me. And then I'll look into contacting Chloe's mother at the VCCW."

He straightened away from the door. His volume raised a notch as the cop resurrected itself and a bit of temper seeped into his tone. "The Virginia Correctional Center for Women? She's in prison? You have no business going there. Let the cops handle the notification. Deputy Cobb seems to like running things."

Laura patted his chest, hushing him before he woke any of her neighbors. "I want to do it. Chloe mentioned her mom when she called me, although I didn't understand exactly what she was saying. Maybe it'd comfort her mother to share my condolences. And then she might be willing to tell me why something like this would happen to her daughter."

"Let the investigators handle it. If you think

there's any connection between Chloe's murder and her mom's crimes, stay out of it. I don't want to see you caught in the middle of something the way Chloe must have been."

"Aww, Detective Wildman really does care," Laura teased, sliding her fingers down the lapels of his coat to poke his stomach. But her laughter quickly faded, and she curled her fingers into her palm feeling singed. That felt like a caress. Of course, he worked out. His chest was hard and muscled. And there was certainly no Pillsbury Doughboy to those abs. She really should stop touching him because even the familiar fist bumps and nudges they'd exchanged for years were colored with the feelings that simmered too close to the surface tonight.

Besides, she wasn't the only one not laughing. "I'm not kidding, Squirt. A woman was murdered. All signs indicate that she fought with her attacker. And lost. I know you feel responsible because she reached out to you, but stay out of this. Don't go looking for trouble." He dropped his hand down to capture hers and pull it back against his chest. He must not feel the same sizzle of electricity between them that she did when they touched. "I'm sorry about your friend."

Laura's eyes instantly felt hot and gritty. Had no one said that to her tonight? There'd been worry and shock and anger and cops and weariness. But Conor's whispered condolence finally triggered her grief. "I wish you could have known her. You would have come up with every blond joke in the book, but she'd have been laughing right along with you. She was impulsive and absent-minded, but you'd have appreciated Chloe's heart." She sniffed back the tears before they became an embarrassing sob. "You'd have liked her."

"I'm sure I would have."

Laura wiped at the first tears that spilled over. "Good night, Conor. It's been…"

Suddenly, there was a man's handkerchief dabbing at her face. With gentle presses against her cheeks and eyes, Conor surrendered his handkerchief to tears and a smear of mascara. When he touched the tip of her runny nose, she pulled the handkerchief from his fingers and took care of that messy business herself. He didn't retreat one inch from sheltering her in the doorway, protecting her ugly cry face from anyone who might step into the hallway and see her pain. The scene reminded her of one summer when she'd wrecked her bike and had scraped up both knees, an elbow and part of her face her helmet hadn't protected. Conor had gotten off his bike and sat right beside her on the edge of the sidewalk. He'd offered her the sleeve of his T-shirt and a lollipop from his pocket to calm her down until Lisa had returned with their dad to load her and the bike into the car for a trip to the emergency room for stitches in her chin.

She brushed her knuckles against the faint scar that lingered from that day and smiled. Conor had grown older, sexier, perhaps more cynical, but the hero inside him hadn't changed. "It's been really good seeing you again."

"Yeah." Despite the late hour and the ruined handkerchief, he seemed reluctant to leave. Reaching behind him, he pulled a business card out of his wallet and handed it to her. "I'll be in town for a couple of days. If anything else happens, if you need a ride to get your things tomorrow, or you just want to talk about coping with grief, give me a call."

Although she folded the card into her hand with the handkerchief, she relieved him of responsibility. "You don't have to take care of me. You and Lisa aren't together anymore. You have no big-brother obligations toward me."

"I mean it, Laura. This has nothing to do with your sister. Loving her had nothing to do with me caring about you. You always had your own place in my heart." For a split second, his confession caught her off guard. Conor cared about her. But clearly, he meant as a friend, and nothing more special, because he went on. "Be careful. One of those men upstairs tonight could have killed Chloe."

"You mean Vinnie or Isaac?"

"The first suspect cops look at is almost always the boyfriend. Or in her case, *boyfriends*. If the killer thinks Chloe told you something incriminating when she called you…"

That brief glow of hearing she was special to Conor faded with the apprehension of his warning. "You think someone I know killed her?"

"There could be other suspects we don't know about—someone connected to her mom, someone she's worked with, even a third boyfriend who didn't like how she was playing the field. But I doubt it was a random home invasion. Not with the way the evidence is stacking up. The police need to find that envelope and who she mailed it to."

"They need to find that ring."

He nodded. "If it even exists. Vinnie may have made that up as an excuse to get back inside Chloe's apartment to retrieve something he doesn't want the cops to find. There's something going on here we don't yet understand. If you remember anything else Chloe said, or if you see someone sniffing around her apartment who shouldn't be there, or if Isaac or Vinnie or Cobb or anybody gives you any trouble while I'm in town, call me. I don't want you dealing with this on your own."

"You always were my big, badass protector."

He touched the tip of his finger to the scar on her chin, maybe remembering that same day from their childhood. "And you were always a handful who jumped in and did things before you thought through the consequences. You needed someone to look out for you." He pointed into her apartment. "I checked your windows already. Lock the dead bolt behind me, or I'll be camping outside your door."

"Will do. Thank you." There was an awkward moment when Conor extended his hand and she reached out with both of hers. How were they supposed to say goodbye? A handshake? A hug?

Instead of pulling his hand back, he unsnapped the fascinator clipped behind her ear. "You're right about Lisa's fashion sense. I think your sparkly thingie has wilted." He held the droopy feathers and netting in front of her face before tossing it over her head into the apartment. "Never wear anything that silly again."

Her answering laugh stopped up in her throat when he reached for her hair again. This time, he feathered his fingers into the wavy tresses to untangle the strands and smooth them behind her ear. His gaze slipped over to hers, darkened. And when his head dropped toward hers, Laura's stomach knotted with anticipation. His handsome mouth descended, and she braced her hands against his chest, stretching up on tiptoe to meet his kiss.

His firm lips folded over hers. For one endless moment, he simply touched his mouth to hers, warming her skin, heating up something deeper inside. Then he tugged her bottom lip between his and that knot in her stomach loosened with a jolt of desire. Laura mimicked the little tug on his bottom lip. He met her response with another pull of his own, and a tender duel began. They learned the shape and flavor of each other's mouths—a nibble here, the brush of a tongue there.

Laura clutched a fistful of his coat and shirt, her knuckles digging into the hard muscle she'd discovered earlier and leaned into him. With both hands now, Conor stabbed his fingers into her hair, cradling the back of her head, holding her mouth in place beneath his while he explored her lips from corner to corner, from curve to curve. She heard a low-pitched groan from deep in his throat, and he pushed his tongue against the seam of her lips, demanding entrance. She answered with a whimper of pleasure from her own throat as her lips parted and he thrust inside to taste her eager welcome. He was raw, potent heat, and tasted like rich coffee. The stubble of his beard abraded the tender skin of her mouth, reminding her of his utter maleness, even as he soothed each sensitized nerve ending with the healing stroke of his tongue. Since he seemed willing to see where this kiss would take them, Laura slid her tongue alongside his and darted into his mouth. When his teeth gently closed around it, capturing her boldness, she smiled at the thought of Conor trapping her in this embrace.

All the times she'd imagined kissing Conor hadn't prepared her for the real thing. They hadn't prepared her for the tenderness and teasing, the sense of being gently asked and surely taken at the same time. They hadn't prepared her for the thump of his heart beneath her hand or the sound of her own pulse thundering in her ears as he touched her with nothing but his lips and his kneading hands in her hair. This kiss was living up to every fantasy and taking her to a reality that was far more satisfying and maybe even a little bit scarier than her dreams, judging by the mindless way her brain was singing and her common sense was shutting down and her blood was turning to molten want in her veins.

Conor was patient and thorough, sensitive and sexy, familiar and surprising… And he was chuckling deep in his throat as he eased his grip on the back of her head, lowering her heels back to the floor, ending the kiss.

But with his superior height, he still leaned

over her, his blue eyes searching every nuance of her heated face and mussed hair before his gaze locked on to hers. "That's for earlier. You caught me off guard then." His voice was a husky rumble that vibrated against her eardrums and agitated nerve endings that were still firing with the pent-up need that Conor's kiss had finally, fully awakened.

Laura couldn't help holding on tighter to his coat as he pulled his fingers from her hair. He tilted his head at a curious angle and his eyes narrowed, as if he was trying to reconcile kissing her with all the ways he must have kissed her sister. "I think you caught me off guard again," he whispered.

"Is that a bad thing?"

"No." He straightened, and Laura finally gave him the space he needed by releasing him and crossing her arms in front of her. The sun hadn't come up yet on this blustery February morning, and her skin was suddenly awash with goose bumps. "But I'm not sure what to make of it yet. You're not…"

"Lisa?"

"I just never thought…" His shoulders lifted with an apologetic shrug. "It was always her."

She nodded her reluctant acceptance of the facts. "And I remind you of her. That kiss was a trip down memory lane for you."

"No. You're not anything like her. That kiss was nothing like anything she and I ever shared."

But Lisa was the sister he'd loved. She wasn't anything like the woman he could love. "It's okay, Conor. I've just always…wanted to kiss you." That much she would confess. "I knew you'd be good at it. We're cool, though."

He didn't look entirely convinced. "I'm still going to call you Squirt."

The nickname again. That meant he wanted to keep his distance. That truly had been just a kiss for him. He hadn't made any promises. He hadn't started a relationship or traded in old feelings for new ones. Laura needed to dial back the hope that had swelled inside her by several notches. So, she teased him the way a little girl with scraped knees and a teenager with wounded pride would. She retreated a step into the apartment, putting some space between them. "Stubborn much?"

He tucked a finger under her chin to tilt her gaze up to his. "You have no idea." He leaned down and placed a firm peck on her mouth, pulling away before she could respond and misinterpret what *that* kiss meant. "I'll call and check on you later, okay?"

Baby steps, Laura. She'd had half a lifetime to decide how she felt about the boy next door. Conor had just discovered the possibilities between them, and clearly wasn't ready for things to change. Maybe he never would be. But he'd promised that this wasn't goodbye. This was just goodbye for now. She reached for the door and offered him a smile. "Okay. Good night, Conor."

"Good night." She didn't hear him striding away until she'd fastened the dead bolt and chain. Until he knew she was safe. No wonder she'd fallen in love with him.

She spotted the discarded fascinator on the rug where Conor had tossed it and padded across the room to retrieve it. How was she going to get over this if he never gave her a chance? If he never gave love another chance?

Laura was still damp from her shower and smoothing lotion onto her legs when her cell phone rang. She wrapped a towel around her dripping hair, another around her body and hurried into the bedroom to pick her phone up off its charger.

"Yes? Conor?" Her tone was slightly breathless from her dash to pick up the call before it went to voice mail. When no one immediately answered, she realized she hadn't paused to read the caller ID. Had she foolishly hoped that Conor was calling to check on her one more time before he grabbed some sleep, too? "Hello?" She could tell there was someone on the line. She could hear jazz music playing faintly in the background. Underneath the sound of someone exhaling in deep, measured breaths. "Is this a butt dial? A wrong number? Who are you trying to reach?" No answer. "I'm going to hang up."

"I wouldn't do that if I were you, Laura." The evenly modulated voice spoke in such a soft whisper she could barely make out the words over the music. Not a wrong number. Not a mistake. He knew her name. "Who is this? I'll trace your number as soon as I hang up. I'll report you to the police for harassment."

"Bold words for a dead woman."

She sank onto the edge of the bed, her knees suddenly too shaky to stand. "What do you mean?"

The ominous chill in every syllable left her shaking. "The truth can get you killed. How much do you know? What did the dead girl tell you?"

Chapter Six

Conor climbed out of his SUV as Laura pulled up in her car in the visitors' parking lot at the Virginia Correctional Center for Women. The light flurries of snow falling from the gray afternoon sky hadn't stopped her from coming. His warning hadn't stopped her, either. He grumbled a mixture of worry and frustration as he buttoned up his winter coat over his sweater and jeans, and tucked his scarf inside the collar. "I knew you weren't going to let this go."

He was standing at the driver's side door, waiting for her with his arms folded across his chest when she finally turned off the engine and got out. She didn't even have the good grace to look apologetic when she tilted her gaze up to his. "Why are you here?" she asked, pulling a knit cap on over her hair.

"Because I knew you'd come, and I'm here to stop you."

Laura closed the door and locked her car. "It's just a conversation with my friend's mother."

"In. Over. Your. Head."

She mirrored his stance, arms crossed to match her defiant tone. "I'm not a little girl anymore. I've been here before with Chloe. I just want to understand what happened to my friend. And why some guy would…" She flicked away the flakes of snow clinging to the sleeve of her coat and stepped up onto the sidewalk without finishing her sentence.

"Some guy would what?" In a single step, Conor was at her side. He knew stalling when he saw it. "Did something else happen?"

She glared holes into the middle of his chest when she stopped. No eye contact. Great. He wasn't going to like this. "I got a phone call. Early this morning, not too long after you left. I couldn't tell who it was.There was too much background noise, and he was speaking softly—probably at a bar. Probably drunk. Probably nothing. Except—" now she met his gaze "—he knew my name."

A tickle of stone-cold suspicion raised the hairs on the back of his neck. "What did he say?"

"He wanted to know what the dead girl told me."

"He thinks Chloe told you something?" She nodded. "Did he threaten you?"

"His threat didn't mean anything."

So, he had. "It meant something to him. *Dead girl?* He used those exact words? Sounds like he was dropping a pretty clear hint."

Laura shook her head at his assessment and started walking again. "I don't know what Chloe was talking about on the phone. It was so hushed, so much gibberish. What if she was already hurt? What if she was already dying when she called me? Maybe that's why she didn't make any sense. She said *insurance*. What kind of insurance? I have no idea what it is or where it is."

"This guy might think she gave it to you. He could be watching your place. Watching you."

"You're being paranoid." She climbed the steps to the visitors' entrance.

"And you're not. But you should be." He paused at the foot of the concrete steps, scanning the parking lot for anyone or any vehicle that seemed out of place. A couple of cop cars, prison vehicles, unmarked cars that could belong to staff, visitors or even some of the prisoners themselves. It was too cold for anyone to wait in their cars without running the heater, and he'd see the exhaust. The pristine perfection of a tranquil Sunday afternoon shouldn't have worried him as much as it did. All the more reason to follow Laura up the steps. "If somebody is out to get you, he will get to you unless you're being hypervigilant. Or you're in witness protection."

She halted on the upper sidewalk and spun around. Her pointed look stopped him two steps below her, putting them nearly at eye level. "You think I need to ask for witness protection? Do I fit some profile from your old job with the Feds? I don't know anything." She gestured to the brick building behind her. "That's why I'm here. To find out information."

He counted the three snowflakes that landed on her cheeks and melted into her freckles, giving himself a moment to tone down the gloom and doom. "Maybe I'm overreacting. That's just the way my brain's hard-wired. When you're responsible for someone's life, you see the enemy everywhere."

She took his gloved hand in hers. "Well, now that you've got me thoroughly freaked out, would you help me instead of scaring me? Would you come inside and talk to Verna Wilson with me? The detective in you wants answers—I know he does. That's really why you're here, right? To talk to Chloe's mom?"

"I'm here to keep you from doing something crazy. Let Cobb and his team run the investigation. He was right about one thing. Protecting people is what I'm good at. I don't want to see you get hurt."

"Then protect me. I'm going in there whether you like it or not. I'd rather have you watching my back than being mad at me."

"I'm not mad."

She was winning this argument. She already knew she was staying and that he was staying with her. "You're just going all big brother on me again?"

More snowflakes hit her upturned face, and he had the strangest urge to brush them away with his fingertip. Or his lips. What was wrong with him? He'd never had these randy impulses with Lisa. Everything between them had been planned, predictable, a slow build leading up to the passion. With Lisa, he'd had time to think. Every move with Laura seemed to be...reacting. As if he couldn't help himself around her. Apparently, he couldn't because he heard himself admitting, "I wasn't thinking brotherly thoughts when I was kissing you earlier."

"Kind of messes with the status quo, doesn't it? To see each other as different people than we were growing up." She smiled, arching her mouth into a bow that was every bit as pinup-worthy as the decadent curves of her jeans.

An instant stab of pure male heat fired through his blood and sent his brain south of his belt buckle.

"The status quo is overrated." Obeying the errant impulse, he leaned forward to kiss her. Laura's sexy mouth softened like a sigh beneath his. The cool leather of her gloved fingers came up to cup his jaw and hold his lips against hers. And for one insane second, he wondered if the rest of her body would be equally responsive to his touch.

But the moment he imagined his hands on her breasts, her body naked beneath his, the reality of what he was thinking jolted through him like an electric shock, and he pulled away. It didn't help that her changeable eyes had darkened like jade flecked with shards of gold, and she looked like she was a witch who'd known exactly what he'd been thinking. Like she'd been the one to put those impetuous thoughts in his head.

Sex with Laura was off the table. Kissing her should be, too. He shouldn't be feeling these restless impulses inside him, either. He was going back to Kansas City. He was leaving this life behind. He wasn't good relationship material, and he'd be damned if he hurt one of his best friends by succumbing to some sort of love-'em-and-leave-'em fling just to get this unexpected attraction out of his system.

Conor inhaled a deep breath of the chilly winter air and forced himself to remember why he was here in the first place. To find answers. To protect Laura from her own curiosity and compassion. That was something he could allow himself to do. He grasped her hand, pulling her into step beside him. "Come on. Let's get this over with. And then you're going to tell me everything about that phone call."

A few minutes later, the guard behind the sign-in counter smiled in recognition as he pushed the clipboard toward Conor. "Marshal Wildman. Long time, no see."

Conor unholstered his service Glock and set it on the counter beside the smaller Beretta he wore in the holster around his ankle. "Pete. How are the grandkids?"

"Growing up too fast. You're not hunting for a fugitive today, are you?" The older man with the shiny bald pate raised his right hand. "I swear we've got everyone locked up where they should be."

Conor grinned before pulling his badge and laying it on the counter, too. "I'm not in the business anymore. Moved to Kansas City, Missouri, a couple of years ago to work with the police department there. I'm here with a friend." He nodded toward Laura, who was already moving through the metal detector on this side of the waiting area leading into the visitation room. "We're here to see Verna Wilson."

Pete raised his shaggy white brows. "She's a popular lady today."

"What do you mean?" Conor removed his cell

phone and watch and set them on the counter with the rest of his belongings.

"Considering visiting hours are restricted, you're already the…" He flipped back through the signatures on his chart, counting names. "You're the fourth person to come in to see Verna today. Must be a case breaking wide open."

"Her daughter was murdered last night."

The guard frowned, offering a moment of sympathy before dropping Conor's things into a large envelope and sticking a label on it. "Sucks to be her today. Are your lady friend and Verna close?"

"She was good friends with Verna's daughter. I don't suppose you'd tell me who else has been in to see her?"

"You know I can't do that unless you have a court order, or I get word from the warden." He pointed toward the waiting area. "But there's one of her guests coming out now."

He turned to see T. J. Cobb trading a joke with the guard at the steel lockdown door. He was probably here making the death notification.

"Thanks, Pete." Conor waved a goodbye and hurried through the metal detector to stand beside Laura. When he protectively slid his hand against the small of her back, she startled, and he knew she wasn't any happier to see the deputy here than he was.

"What are you doing here, Detective?" Cobb's

smile was big and friendly and fake as he greeted them. "Miss Karr with a K." He winked. "Where's the pink dress?"

Laura stiffened against Conor's hand. "We're here to extend our condolences to Chloe's mother."

"I was just paying my respects myself."

Conor doubted his visit had been a social call. "Did you ask if her daughter's death could have been retaliation for something she might have done?"

"*My* investigation, Wildman." Cobb tipped his hat without answering Conor's question. "You folks have a nice day." He headed toward the front desk. "Pete. When is your wife going to bake me another one of her apple pies?"

Once Cobb had left the waiting area, Laura muttered under her breath, "I don't know if it's his patronizing 'little woman' teasing or his bully-with-a-badge condescension that makes me not like that guy."

"I think it's just because he's mean and stupid," Conor deadpanned.

She laughed, easing some of the wary tension roiling inside him, too. "Thanks. I needed that. Let's go on in."

Conor and Laura were sitting on stools that were bolted to the floor in the visitation room when a guard escorted Verna Wilson in and sat her at the table across from them. Clearly, the fortysomething woman—with gaunt cheeks, yellowed teeth and a nervous habit of drumming her fingers on the thighs of her scrubs-like uniform, indicating her history of drug use and recovery—had gotten the news of her daughter's murder. Although she barely registered an emotion one way or the other on her face, her sunken eyes, red and puffy, were evidence of the tears she'd shed.

"Chloe was beautiful and talented and fun to hang out with." Laura was trying to establish a rapport with the older woman so that she'd open up and talk. Since Verna had already recognized him as law enforcement, and barely made eye contact with him, Conor let Laura build that connection. "I'm so sorry, Mrs. Wilson. No one should have to die like that."

"Sounds like she crossed the wrong people."

"You mean the wrong man. Her attack was very…personal, I think."

"Sure. Whatever." Verna's fingers moved their incessant tapping to the top of the table when she leaned forward to whisper. "Look, I'm here because I crossed the wrong people. That's dangerous business."

Laura clasped her hands in her lap, no doubt resisting the urge to reach out and still those fingers. "Chloe said you'd been arrested for selling drugs."

"Yeah. The people I worked for didn't appreciate that I was skimming some of the product for my own use. They ratted me out." Verna exchanged a look with the guard at the door and sat back. "I was on parole. It was my third offense. I'm doing my time."

"Couldn't you report those people?" Laura suggested. "Testify against them for a lighter sentence?"

Verna laughed at her hopeful naïveté. "Being stuck in here a few more years is better than being dead. It's better than my Chloe being dead."

"They threatened her to keep you quiet?"

"Back when I first got arrested." Her fingers stilled into a fist. "But she was a kid then. And I've been silent as the grave. I never mentioned one name. Not a peep. Whoever killed my girl is something different. It's not on me."

"Something different than the drug dealer you worked for? Did she ever mention insurance to you? Do you have any ideas? Can you tell the police anything?"

"Not if I want to stay alive in here." Verna warned her, her gaze darting to Conor to include him, too. "Be smart and let it go. Chloe had a good thing, but she ruined it because she wanted more. She couldn't leave well enough alone."

"So, she did talk to you about it." Laura pushed. "What good thing? What did she ruin?"

"A real relationship."

"With Isaac Royal or Vinnie Orlando?"

Verna didn't answer.

Conor prodded her for a response to an easier question that didn't involve naming murder suspects. "Besides Deputy Cobb, who's been here to see you today?"

She was drumming again. Maybe that nervous tic was less about combatting her need for a fix, and more about controlling the urge to answer their questions.

After receiving a nod of permission from the guard, Verna pushed to her feet. "Time's up. I gotta go."

"Verna, please. Anything you can do to help us…" Laura shot to her feet to stop her, but Conor grabbed her arm and pulled her back to the table, preventing her from touching the prisoner. That didn't stop her plea, though. "I don't want Chloe's killer to get away with murder."

The older woman stopped for one last word. "Chloe was messing with people who don't like to be messed with. And as much as I loved her, she was trash, just like me. No amount of money can ever change that."

"She wasn't trash. You aren't. Verna?"

The guard unlocked the door, then Verna re-entered the cellblock without ever looking back.

Night rolled in with a blanket of clouds that reflected the lights of the city back onto the snow, creating an eerie brightness over the stillness of the cemetery where his mother was buried. The hazy light also created impenetrable shadows behind every tombstone, tree and mausoleum. There were plenty of places for an enemy to lie in wait, or a spy to chart their movements without anyone ever knowing they were here. Conor had a bad feeling that someone *was* out there, tracking Laura's every move.

It wasn't the first time in the past twenty-four hours that he'd sensed someone watching them. If he wasn't with her, would that someone do more to Laura than just watch?

Conor squeezed his fingers around the steering wheel, replaying everything Laura had told him. Some anonymous rat had called her and threatened to kill her if she didn't tell him everything she knew about Chloe's secrets.

With one woman already dead, he didn't think it was an idle threat.

He followed the winding road through the iron gates and around the first hill, keeping Laura and her car squarely in his rearview mirror. He wanted her here in the SUV with him. Partly so he knew she was safe from crank phone calls and pompous deputies who didn't care a fig for her safety, but also because he liked hanging out with her. She was funny and sexy and smelled like an exotic perfume that was unique from any other woman's. She was clever. She kept him on his toes. She was every bit as impulsive and driven by her emotions as she'd been growing up. But what had once been a source of frustration and amusement, he now saw as something intriguing. Enticing. Hell, if she wasn't Lisa's little sister, and this attraction he felt didn't seem so awkward, he'd be asking her out. No, he'd be asking her *in*. For the evening. Maybe for the whole night. This trip home to Arlington had taken a completely unexpected turn—and it wasn't just because he and Laura had discovered a woman's dead body.

He pulled up beside the grove of evergreens that marked the hilltop where his parents rested for eternity, killed the engine and got out to meet Laura before she parked behind him and climbed out of her car.

"I wasn't counting on the sun to set so early," he apologized, holding the door open for her. "The gates won't close for another twenty minutes or so. We'll make this quick, I promise."

"Take your time." She zipped up her short jacket before nudging him back a step, as if his protective stance was crowding her. Or maybe she just needed a better angle to tilt her gaze up to his. "Checking to make sure your mother's marker is set correctly and is exactly how you ordered it is important." Her palm lingered at the middle of his chest. He liked that she was a toucher. He liked that a lot. "That would have been ridiculous to drive me all the way across the city and then double back to the cemetery. And I wouldn't have felt right, leaving my car unattended in the prison parking lot overnight. Besides, I'd like to pay my respects to Marie."

"I would have been happy to take you home and do this tomorrow," he repeated, just like he'd offered outside the women's prison. "It's not like Mom's going anywhere."

She patted his chest before circling the car and leading the way to his mother's stone. She *had* been here to pay her respects before. He liked that about Laura a lot, too. Damn it. Conor's frustrated huff clouded the cold air around him. He needed to stop making a list of Laura Karr pros and cons—not that he could come up with a single con at the moment. Except maybe this propensity to get involved with some dangerous people.

She was his friend. She needed his law enforcement expertise to help her navigate this unofficial investigation into her friend's murder. She wanted him to watch her back. Period.

His gaze dropped to the sweet flare of her hips

walking away from him. Nope, he had absolutely no problem watching her backside.

He squeezed his eyes shut, silently reprimanding himself on the errant thought. *Hopeless, Wildman. You're hopeless.*

He hurried the last few yards to catch up to Laura, reaching her as she stooped down to brush the fresh snow off the red marble marker. He stood above her, still feeling that clutch of grief in his gut as he read his mother's name and the dates of her birth and death, and saw the spray of daffodils etched into the stone's polished finish. "It looks perfect. Simple and beautiful. Marie would have approved."

Although the grass wouldn't fill in around the newly placed headstone until spring, he was happy to see that the monument matched his expectations. "The daffodils were her request before she died. She always had them growing in the backyard."

"I remember. All around the fence. They'd bloom every spring." Laura reached up to squeeze his hand before pulling herself up beside him. Then she hooked her free hand around the sleeve of his coat and rested her head against his shoulder in another one of those arm hugs that made him lean a little closer to her, too. It took him a few moments longer to exit his thoughts and realize that Laura was switching topics. "Who calls her own daughter trash?"

Obviously, she'd been stewing over her friend's murder and not fixating on him the way he'd spent every mile thinking about her. It was almost a relief to switch gears from trying to make sense of the relationship he couldn't have and start making sense about Chloe Wilson's murder. His mother's new stone, and the older, weathered slab of marble beside it gave him the explanation he needed. "Not every family looks like the cover of a magazine. A lot of us don't grow up with a Ron and Leslie Karr like you did."

Her fingers tightened around his hand and arm. "You're talking about your father now, aren't you." She looked down at Arthur Wildman's gravestone before glancing up at him. "Did he denigrate you like that?"

"Nah. He wasn't around enough to screw me up that way." Although stepping up to be the man of the house at the ripe old age of eight—when Arthur was accidentally electrocuted at work two years after abandoning his family—had instilled in Conor a rigid sense of responsibility and equipped him with a sarcastic armor. His father's death had ended any shred of hope Conor had nursed about his family reuniting, and the defensive shield kept most people at a far enough distance so he couldn't be hurt again. "I have some good memories of him from when I was little," he admitted. "I remember him holding me up on his shoulders to watch a parade. He was as tall as I am now. It felt like flying to be lifted so high. I think I was about four. Soon after that, he just wasn't there."

"We're your family." Conor remembered running after his father as he tossed a duffel bag packed with his personal belongings into the back of his truck. Conor's skin had chapped with all the tears he'd cried that day. *"I'm your son."*

"It's not enough," Arthur answered. *"You go on back in the house with your mom. And stop that cryin'. You'll be okay."*

But he hadn't been. Maybe a part of him still wasn't. "He didn't want to be tied down to us, to the responsibilities of raising a son and supporting a family and living in suburbia. A couple years later he was dead."

Laura's hold on him shifted and she sidled even closer, circling her arms around his waist and resting her cheek against his heart. "I can't imagine what it would feel like to be abandoned like that. But you had your mom. Marie was as solid and hardworking as they come."

Conor stared down at the gravestone, finding solace in the squeeze of Laura's arms, in the scent of her warming the cold air he breathed, in the unabashed way she aligned her strong, short body against his. Her words reminded him of better times. Her compassion spread a balm over the raw wounds inside him. It felt completely natural, if not necessary, to wind his arms around her and settle his chin on the crown of her knit cap. "I was lucky to have her."

"We all were."

He could even look over at his father's marker and remember everything he admired about the woman who'd raised him. "They never got divorced. Mom took care of the funeral arrangements when he died—I guess she still loved him."

"Or it was her sense of duty. I mean, you've got that in spades—it had to come from somewhere."

"Maybe." He wasn't sure how long they stood there together, but it wasn't long enough before Laura was pulling away. "Cold?"

She shook her head, even as she hugged her arms around her own waist against the chilly air. Maybe she was as uncomfortable with the changing dynamics of their relationship as he was. Maybe a cemetery after dusk wasn't the place to be thinking about relationship dynamics at all.

Relationship dynamics. Conor shook off the longing that holding Laura stirred inside him. She needed a cop, not a rehash of his sorry life history. And the cop in him suddenly had a pretty clear insight into Chloe Wilson. "Verna might have been onto something about Chloe."

"What do you mean?"

"She said Chloe had a *good thing,* but that she got greedy. She wanted more."

Laura shrugged, not yet catching his train of thought. "More what? Money? She was making some money with her ceramics at art shows, paid the regular bills with waitressing. She always seemed to have a boyfriend who'd take care of anything else."

"You know what a kid from a broken family wants more than anything? More than money?" He held out his hand, waiting for Laura to take it. "A family that isn't broken. Security. It's probably why she liked having you as a friend—you were loyal and reliable, an anchor she could count on in her life. If she was involved with someone, she'd want that guy to commit."

Laura's fingers closed around his as understanding dawned. "You think she was blackmailing Vinnie into marrying her?"

He shortened his stride and she fell into step beside him. "Maybe he gave her a ring. Then decided killing her was the only way to make sure she kept his secret."

They retraced their path through the snow back to their cars. "What secret? She never told me anything."

"There are plenty of skeletons people hide in their closets. Things that could hurt them emotionally. Things that are bad for business or someone's reputation. Things that could land them in jail. Or get them killed."

"But how would Chloe find out anything so incriminating? She was hardly a detective."

"Pillow talk?"

"Maybe it wasn't Vinnie she was blackmailing. It could have been Isaac. He said she showed him that envelope." Laura pulled out her keys and tapped the remote to unlock her car. When nothing happened, she muttered a curse and used the key. Conor silently vowed to find some time in his day tomorrow to get her car to the dealership to either replace the battery or reprogram the remote. "Maybe she threatened to expose him somehow if he didn't stay away—didn't let her marry Vinnie. You saw his hand. Maybe yesterday wasn't the first time he lost his temper with her. Instead of reporting the incident to the cops, she used the information to get him to leave her alone."

"Sounds like we've got several possibilities. We need to find that envelope." Conor opened the door for her.

Instead of climbing in, Laura stopped with the door between them and faced him. "We? Are you sticking around for a while, after all?"

If she smiled at him like that every day and kissed him like she had at her apartment every night, it'd be hard to walk away. But he knew better than to promise any kind of forever. "Long enough. For as long as I can before I have to report back to work in Kansas City."

Her smile dimmed. "I wish you would stay."

"I don't think I could be happy here anymore. I've got a new life I'm anxious to get back to."

"Are you running to a new life? Or running away from your old one?"

That observation made him feel a little like his father. And that wasn't a very comfortable comparison to make. "You don't mince words, do you, Squirt." His deep breath clouded the air between them for a moment. "You're a lot like Lisa in that regard."

"You said I wasn't anything like her." Her forehead puckered with a frown, and her pinkie brushed against his where they rested their hands on top of the door. With them both wearing gloves, he shouldn't be able to feel her touch. And yet he seemed hyperaware of every move she made, every nuance of her expression. Comparing her to Lisa worried her somehow. "I don't want you to think of me as a carbon copy of the woman who hurt you. I don't want you to see the girl I used to be. I want you to just see me."

"That honesty must be a Karr quality." Conor hooked his pinkie around hers, completing the link she'd been hesitant to make, assuring her that nothing Lisa had said or done would ever impact the friendship between him and Laura. "Trust me, you are one of a kind. You're shorter and curvier than your sister. But it's not just your looks. You're more impulsive than Lisa. You have a big heart. You're loaded with compassion."

"Lisa has a big heart, too."

He shook his head. "She's afraid to use it. I've got no doubt that she loves Joe. And I think she had genuine feelings for me. But…she's not willing to risk putting herself out there unless she can control all the possible outcomes. I wasn't something she could control. Not with the hours I had to keep. Not with the lies I had to tell to protect my witnesses."

"Now you're back to thinking I'm foolish again. Because I put myself out there. I get involved with things I shouldn't."

"I think you're incredibly brave to follow your heart. To take chances on caring about people, and to risk getting hurt." He steepled her fingers with his before lacing their fingers together and squeezing her hand. "I haven't been that kind of brave for a while."

"Conor…"

No. He was going to say this. "The guy who gets you—the one who captures that heart—he'll be a lucky man."

"What if I told you…?" Whatever she'd been

about to confess was interrupted by the phone ringing in her car. "There is a guy who..."

The phone demanded her attention. "You'd better get that."

With a heavy sigh, she pulled away and reached inside to the passenger seat to retrieve her phone from her purse. "Hello? Yes? I understand. No, I won't forget." Although he couldn't make out the words, Conor could tell it was a man's voice. When she sank onto the seat behind the steering wheel, as if the wind had been knocked out of her, he came around the door to kneel in front of her. "I said I would. Do you have any idea...? Hello?"

Something was wrong. Was that rat coward calling to threaten her again? "Laura? Who is it?"

The caller had hung up. She hugged the phone to her chest. "Deputy Cobb. He said they found a receipt from the post office in Chloe's apartment that matches the package she sent out. Like you said, he thinks it could be the key to breaking open his investigation. It should be delivered tomorrow."

"Did they track who she sent the package to?" Laura nodded. "Me."

Chapter Seven

"Yes, ma'am." Laura leaned forward to update the information on her computer. "I've added the extra room for the new chaperones and confirmed their flights. Looks like the Chapman Middle School is all set for their DC tour over spring break." Once she submitted the revised travel package to her office and printed off a copy for her own files, she turned her cell off speakerphone and put it up to her ear to complete the call. "Have a safe trip from Nebraska."

While she pulled the papers off the printer tray with her left hand, she opened the top drawer with her right and reached inside for the stapler. It was an action she'd done a hundred times. But her fingertips hit a box of paper clips and a tray of highlighters, instead, forcing her to actually look into the drawer. She opened it a few more inches and saw that the stapler had gotten pushed behind her other office supplies. "There you are. How did you get back there?"

One more mystery she couldn't solve. Just like the question about what Chloe could have sent her in the mail. And where was the postman, already?

After stapling the papers together and moving the stapler back to its rightful spot, Laura crossed her booted feet on the leather ottoman beside her desk and let her eyes drift shut. Typically, she caught up on phone calls and paperwork on the days she worked from home. And though the jeans and old college sweatshirt she wore were a lot more comfortable than the starched petticoat and layers of lace and tulle she'd worn most of the weekend, she felt off this morning. Kind of like that stapler. Exhaustion had claimed her for about five hours of dreamless sleep last night. But by 4:00 a.m., she'd been tossing and turning.

Now she was having trouble focusing on anything job-related. She'd sat at the breakfast table, trying to pinpoint a smell in her apartment, something musky and cloying, but so indistinct that she must be imagining it. Could a person imagine smells? Eating her oatmeal with her eyes closed and her brain half asleep, she decided the scent was somebody's aftershave. But Conor and her dad were the only men who'd been in the apartment recently. Her father was an Old Spice guy and Conor smelled…like Conor. This was woodsy…no, floral…no, a figment of her imagination. She'd gone through a pot of coffee after that, then had brewed a second one just to keep the smell of the steaming, fragrant java in the apartment, dulling her scent receptors to the idea of invisible men and nonexistent aftershave.

Diving into her to-do list hadn't distracted her much. She had opened her email to tackle a couple of work projects. Laura was physically drained from the wedding and Chloe's death, along with the sleepless night that had followed. Last night simply hadn't been enough to catch up. More than that, her thoughts kept slipping away from processing tour packages for her clients and ending up fantasizing about Conor kissing her again. Or worrying about Conor. He seemed so melancholy when they'd visited his parents' graves. He'd seemed so alone.

How could a man who was so good at making people laugh, so good at making her feel safe and cared for, so good at keeping bullies and bad guys in line, be so isolated? Coming home to Arlington had forced him to face down his past and all the things that had hurt him. He had friends, but no family. He'd overcome the tragedy of losing his mother and growing up without his father. He'd moved beyond Lisa ending their relationship and marrying his college roommate. But at what cost?

The man she'd held at the cemetery needed to be loved. He needed to know that there were relationships in this world that lasted. He needed to trust that his love would be safe with someone else—with her, she hoped. But how did she break through that hard wall of armor around his heart and convince him of that? Was she even the right woman to do it? She wanted to try. For Conor, for her own future, she really wanted to try.

She'd nearly blurted out her feelings last night at the cemetery, just before Deputy Cobb's call. That probably would have ended up in another humiliating moment followed by a few jokes to make light of her confession and allow them to pretend a declaration of love hadn't happened. Then Conor would go home and stew about it, probably feeling guilty that he'd inspired an affection he couldn't return, and she would go home and...

Laura's eyes popped open. Spend the day wanting and wishing and not having any clue how to make him see that he fell for the wrong sister. She dropped her feet to the floor and stood. Why did she feel like there was a deadline for her to get Conor to wake up and see her as the right woman for him? And just how selfish was she to keep pushing him out of his comfort zone when he seemed to need a friend more than anything else right now?

Laura shook her head and picked up her coffee mug before heading to the kitchen. She had plenty to worry about right now, without throwing her feelings for Conor into the mix. She stopped at the window over the sink and peeked through the blinds for the mail truck. She wasn't the only one impatient for the mail to arrive. Across the street, a little way down the block, there was a black and white car from the sheriff's department. Either Deputy Cobb or one of his coworkers had been parked down there since breakfast, waiting for Chloe's package to be delivered.

Needing something mindless to do instead of thinking and waiting, she opened a can of soup to warm on the stove. Then she sat down to pick at her lunch. Was Conor eating lunch, too? Did he do simple things like eat three meals a day to take care of himself? Or was he too busy meeting with the furnace guy at his mother's house to take care of that responsibility, and calling some old friends in local law enforcement to try to find out whatever he could about Chloe and Verna Wilson, Isaac Royal and Vinnie Orlando? He'd promised to share any information he uncovered, even as he'd reminded her to keep her nose out of the murder investigation once she received Chloe's package and turned it over to Deputy Cobb.

She spotted the white mail truck in front of her building when she carried her dishes to the sink. A sense of anticipation coiled through her. Was that package the answer to Chloe's murder? Was a voice from the grave about to reveal her killer's identity? Were the threatening phone calls and wary suspicions about the danger Chloe had gotten involved with about to end? Laura scooped up her phone and texted Conor to let him know the package had arrived. Then she grabbed her keys and hurried out the door.

She reached the lobby and wall of mailboxes in time to wave a goodbye to the letter carrier on his way out the front doors. Ignoring the beep of Conor's reply, and the blast of cold air that made her shiver, she inserted the key into the lock and pulled open her box. Her breath stopped up in her chest when she saw the padded white envelope folded in half and stuffed inside. Eager to find answers as much as she dreaded discovering what those answers were, she pulled out the envelope, leaving the rest of her mail in the box.

There was the red lipstick mark. Definitely from Chloe. She trailed her fingers across her name written in her friend's artistic scrawl and felt a pang of sorrow over the loss of such talent, such zest for living, such a generous free spirit that had all been violently taken from the world.

"Is that it?"

Laura shied away from the growly, good ol' boy voice that startled her. She turned with her back against the mailboxes and looked up at T. J. Cobb, who was knocking snow from the sleeves of his uniform jacket.

She let the wintry air he'd brought in with him settle around her before she spoke. "I said I'd bring it to you as soon as it arrived. What if there's something personal inside?"

"What if there's evidence for my investigation?"

She hugged the envelope to her chest. "It's my mail. You can't take it unless you have a warrant."

"I thought you understood how this was gonna work when we talked last night. A warrant takes time. Don't you want me to find your friend's killer?"

"Of course I do."

He took a step toward her. "Then you'd better open it and see what's inside."

"With you looking over my shoulder?"

He was staring right at her. Waiting to grab whatever Chloe had entrusted her with. "How do I know you're not going to hide something you might find in there unless I'm right here with you?" He took off his hat and knocked it against his thigh, adding to the puddle of melting snow forming at his feet. "I'd be happy to come up to your place and open it in private, if you prefer."

In private? Alone with Deputy Slimeball? She wished now that she'd taken a few minutes to wait for Conor to get here before coming downstairs. Although she had a disturbing feeling Deputy Cobb would have been knocking at her apart-

ment door to make her come down to the mailboxes the moment the delivery had been made.

"Fine." With her back literally against the wall,
she had nowhere to go, anyway. Even with his
lumbering weight, she had a feeling the deputy
moved faster than he spoke. There wasn't any
place she could run to before he caught up with
her. And the idea of him putting those big bear
paws on her to stop her made her stomach churn.
"I'll open it."

With that announcement, she unfolded the envelope and smoothed it against her thigh. A blip
of confusion distracted her for a moment. Hadn't
Isaac said something about the envelope being
lumpy? Not only were there no lumps between
the padded sides, but it felt as though there might
not be anything at all inside.

"Today?" Cobb reminded her of his hovering
presence and her need to get rid of him as soon
as possible.

She inhaled a deep breath to calm her nerves,
and for a split second, she was breathing air
tainted with the deputy's scent. Her nose stung
with the unpleasant tang of sweat masked by
Deputy Cobb's cologne.

Or aftershave.

Laura averted her gaze, trying to match his
scent to the one she'd imagined earlier in her
apartment. She certainly hadn't imagined body

odor, and his aftershave or body spray or whatever application he thought made him smell better was more potent than the smell she'd talked herself out of identifying. She didn't think T. J. Cobb had been inside her apartment while she'd been out with Conor, or worse, while she'd been asleep in her bed.

But someone had.

She hadn't imagined anything.

A new wave of fear washed over her, leaving her shaking. A stranger had been in her home, and she hadn't heard him, hadn't seen any evidence of a forced lock or broken window. She had no idea why someone would break in. Unless he was looking for something. Or looking for her.

"Miss Karr?" The deputy's gloved hand closed over her shoulder, and she couldn't stop herself from bolting at his touch.

"Don't touch me!"

He rested his arms on the holster and handcuffs box anchored to his utility belt. "You went away to la-la land. I do have other responsibilities in this county besides waitin' for you to open the damn envelope."

There was nothing relaxed or friendly about his tone and posture, and Laura didn't pretend she could relax or be polite, either. Without wasting another moment, she slipped her finger beneath the envelope flap and ripped open the sticky seal. She found nothing but a sheet of white paper, which she pulled out. Before reading what was written on the paper, she thrust her hand inside. "There's nothing else in here."

"Are you sure?" Cobb snatched the envelope from her, turning it upside down to dump the contents into his hand.

Just as she'd said, there was nothing there to fall out. "What were you expecting to find?"

"Don't you worry your pretty little head about that," he answered, rolling the envelope into a baton and squeezing it in his fist. "What does that say?"

Laura turned the paper over to find more of Chloe's loopy, colorful handwriting. The fourth sentence after her name had been crossed out. After that, the black ink changed to a crayon-thick green, as if her pen had run out of ink and she'd picked up one of her pastels to finish the note. Or someone had interrupted her, and she had to finish the missive in secret, with whatever instrument she could find.

Laura,
I'm going for the brass ring. I'm going to be happy. I finally figured out how to make the right man love me.
~~*Keep an eye on this*~~
Watch my cat for me. Keep her safe.
Love ya,
Chloe

Cobb shifted to read the letter beside her. "That mean anything to you?"

Laura could honestly shake her head no. She handed the note over to the deputy. "Sounds like she's talking about eloping with Vinnie Orlando. You might as well take it. Maybe there are some fingerprints or something useful you can get off it. I'm sorry the package didn't give you the answers you were looking for. You know, 'Hey, Laura—so and so is trying to kill me.'"

Cobb had no sense of humor. He eyed her suspiciously before replacing the letter in the envelope and stuffing them both inside his jacket. "Why would she write you a letter about taking care of her pet? Why not call? Or run downstairs to ask?"

"Who knows?" Since he didn't ask about the nonexistent feline, Laura didn't volunteer the information. "I was gone a lot this weekend with wedding events." She shrugged at another plausible explanation. "Maybe her phone died." Her memory went back to that last weird phone call with her friend. Her breathless tone. The jazz music in the background. Speaking as if she didn't want someone who was with her to overhear. She pointed to the note he'd tucked away. "That may be old-school communication, but it works. Chloe didn't think like other people."

"It'd be easier if she did."

"Easier to find her killer? The missing ring? Is that what you're looking for?"

The deputy never answered. He put on his hat and touched the brim. "Thank you for your co-operation Miss Karr. Keep *your* phone charged," he advised. "I'll be in touch if I need anything else from you."

Laura watched him get in his patrol car and drive away before she retrieved the rest of her mail and headed upstairs to her apartment.

As soon as she entered her apartment, she closed the door and leaned against it, breathing in deeply, hoping to catch again the faint scent of someone who didn't belong here, so she could try to identify any intruder. But all she could smell was her uneaten vegetable beef soup cooling on the stove. After flipping the dead bolt as well as the knob lock, she moved from room to room, checking behind every blind and curtain for signs of entry. Nothing. Even the snow on the fire escape outside her bedroom window was undisturbed. If there had been an intruder, he'd left no clue behind as to how he'd gotten in or why he'd been here.

Yesterday, Conor had warned her she wasn't being paranoid enough. Today, she was plenty suspicious about every sound, every smell, every threat that she could no longer dismiss as fatigue or imagination. Someone thought she knew something about Chloe's murder. Deputy Cobb seemed to think she knew more than she was telling. The man on the phone thought she knew more.

Fighting the urge to jump into the shower to wash off the scent and touch of T. J. Cobb, Laura sat at her desk and pulled up her emails to see if there was any sort of travel emergency at work, or a funny meme from a friend she could concentrate on. Conor would be here soon, and she didn't want him to worry if he came to the door and she didn't answer because the water was running.

She picked up her phone and read the simple but reassuring text he'd sent her.

On my way.

Smiling at that tiniest of reassurances, she scrolled through the messages in her inbox. Delete. Flag for later. Delete. The messages soon blurred together and became unimportant as she bemoaned Chloe's inability to spell out whatever she meant by insurance. And what was the deal with the cat, anyway?

She'd had plenty of conversations with her friend that had veered from one tangent to another. Discussing a new recipe could turn into talk of a grocery list and morph into a dialogue on the different shades of green in the vegetable world, with Chloe jumping up from the table to grab her box of pastels and sketch out the idea for a jade dragon sculpture with her signature round, owlish features. Laura's gaze drifted to the corner of her desk where she displayed the ceramic dog Chloe had sculpted for her. She loved the warm burgundy color of the glaze, and the rounded, puppy-like expression on his face reminded her of Chloe and made her smile whenever she looked at it.

A jolt of insight straightened Laura's spine. She looked at the little dog again. Chloe made all sorts of animals with those soft, exaggerated features. She sold most of them at art shows. But she'd given Laura a dog that reminded her of the Irish setter she'd had growing up.

And she'd made herself a cat.

The haze of confusion and suspicion that had dulled her thoughts disappeared like the clouds that were breaking up outside, allowing the sun to reflect off the snow and pour through her front window. Laura hurried into the kitchen, peeking through the blinds to ensure Deputy Cobb had gone. With no cop car in sight, she stuffed her phone into her pocket, picked up her keys and ran up the stairs to Chloe's apartment.

Yellow crime scene tape still crisscrossed the doorjamb, but the rectangular seal that bore the official wording that opening this door was illegal had already been sliced through. A part of the seal had been torn off. Was that how the CSI team had left it now that they were done with the apartment? Had someone else, like Vinnie Orlando, already broken in to search the place for himself? Maybe she was too late.

Remembering that Chloe herself had asked her to do this, Laura inhaled a deep breath and inserted her key into the lock.

Ducking beneath the tape, she slipped inside and quickly closed the door behind her. She had to stand there a moment to take control of the grief that swelled up inside her. Little had changed beyond the addition of a few sprinklings of black powder where the crime lab technicians had dusted for fingerprints. The mess in the living room was a haunting reminder that her friend's life had been reduced to trash. She seized upon the anger that followed on the heels of her sorrow and let it give her strength and the determination to get this done.

Moving along the wall as Conor had instructed, she circled the rifled contents of Chloe Wilson's life and went to the bedroom. There were more changes here, although none of them were comforting. The dresser that had rested on top of Chloe's body had been set upright and dusted for prints. And the spot on the rug where Chloe must have taken her last breath had been cut away, probably taken to the lab for analysis. But the exposed bare wood was stained with blood. She idly wondered if the subflooring and support beams held the stains of Chloe's violent death, too.

"Stop it," she whispered to herself. If she let her emotions grab hold of her again, she'd freeze up. Tearing her gaze from the crimson mark on the floor, Laura swept the perimeter of the room until she spotted the blue ceramic cat on Chloe's bedside table. "I'm taking care of the cat, my friend," she muttered, adding a silent prayer that she understood Chloe-speak for *find my insurance and guard it with your life*. Laura had a sinking feeling that that insurance had already cost Chloe hers.

The ceramic creature with the big round eyes and shiny blue glaze was cool to the touch when Laura picked it up and cradled it in her hands. She inspected the sculpture from ears to tail before shaking it. Nothing. It was just a cute little cat made of clay and fired in a kiln.

A cute little cat with a vent hole in the bottom.

Holding the statue to the light seeping in through the bedroom blinds, Laura inspected the hole. There was something stuffed inside the hollow figure. Hopefully, not another cryptic message, although it did look like a wadded-up piece of paper.

I'm not in the mood for a treasure hunt, Chloe.

The hole was just wide enough for Laura to stick her finger inside and work the paper down through the opening. When something inside the paper got stuck, she briefly considered breaking the cat open to retrieve it, but that felt too much like what the killer—who'd tossed this place without any respect for the woman who had owned and cherished these things—would've done.

Instead, Laura tugged on the paper, tearing it bit by bit until only the thing that had been wrapped in it remained inside. Then it was a matter of tilting and jiggling before a tiny black-and-silver flash drive fell into the palm of her hand.

Laura frowned. She'd half expected the heirloom ring Vinnie had been looking for to tumble out. Maybe Conor was right—that story had just been a ruse to get back inside the apartment to find this.

Whatever this was. The thing that Chloe might have been murdered for. Her insurance.

Laura wasn't going to psychically discover what was on the flash drive by holding it in her hand. She needed a computer. When she started to pick up the shreds of paper she'd created, she realized there was another message written on it in black ink. Was this what Chloe had originally planned to send to her, creating the lumpy envelope Isaac had described? What had happened between arguing with Isaac and feeling the need to hide the flash drive? *Who* had happened?

Sparing a few minutes before sneaking out again, Laura stuffed the flash drive into the pocket of her jeans and laid the torn bits of paper on top of the bed, piecing them together like a puzzle until its hidden message revealed itself.

Marry me. Or I'll share this with Mommy.
I don't want to. You know how much I love you. I've got your back on this. But it's time for you to man up and pop the question.
Or I'm sending it to her.
C

Chloe *was* blackmailing somebody. Not Isaac if his story about her dumping him for good the day of the wedding was to be believed.

Vinnie Orlando.

Had Vinnie killed the woman he'd promised to marry?

Who's Mommy? Chloe had always called Verna by her first name when she spoke of her mother— like they were sisters instead of parent and daughter. She'd said *Mommy* during that last phone call, too. Not *Verna*. This was someone else.

I need to get this to Conor. Despite the logic that reminded her she should turn this evidence over to Deputy Cobb, her only thought was to clean up every trace of her being here and get down to her apartment to meet Conor and show him what she'd found. She scooped up the shreds of paper and stuffed them into her pocket before wiping off the cat figurine with the cuffs of her sweatshirt and carefully setting it back in the exact same place on the nightstand, in case the police should come back for another look.

Her phone beeped with a text notification, and she quickly pulled it from her back pocket. Conor must have made great time driving to the outskirts of the city. If he was already at her door, wondering why she wasn't answering his knock, she'd have some awkward explaining to do.

Unable to spend another second in the room where her friend had died, Laura slipped into the hallway and pulled up the message. She'd just be vague and tell him she was on her way, and maybe he wouldn't question how she'd found the flash drive or lecture her about taking risks.

It wasn't Conor.

The entire apartment swirled around her as panic flared inside. But the text on her screen remained crystal clear.

Missing your dead friend, Laura? Find anything?

"How do you know…?" Tearing her focus from the taunting threat, she swept her gaze across the apartment. "Where are you?" Was someone here with her? She hadn't smelled anything out of the ordinary, not even the rotting meat odor she'd half expected to find with all that dried blood. She hadn't heard anything but her own breathing. She hadn't seen...

Her gaze landed on the living room window.

Had those curtains been open the whole time? It had been night when she'd been in here before. But now she could see the snow piling up on the brick sill outside and curling around the corner of the window frame. The blinds were up, the curtains pulled back. Her head swiveled to the front door, then back again. Just like in her apartment, the window was positioned on the far side of the living room, right across from the front door. Could someone have seen her come in? Maybe the spy was out in the hallway.

Conor had warned that she needed to be aware of her surroundings at all times. And she'd just failed big-time.

She wasn't sure if it was morbid curiosity or a stab at survival, but Laura steeled her nerves and forced herself to walk to the window. Keeping as close to the edge of the frame as she could, she peeked outside. She studied the sooty, snow-dusted street below. Had Deputy Cobb returned? There was no official car down there, but that didn't mean he wasn't sitting in an unmarked vehicle. Although most of the residents in the area had driven into the city for work or school for the day, there were still a few cars parked along the sidewalk on either side of the street. Anyone in one of those vehicles could see into the front-facing window, but could they see all the way to the door from that angle? She lifted her gaze to the medical offices and business windows of the buildings across the street. If she could see into their waiting rooms and conference areas, then certainly anyone there could see into Chloe's apartment. They could see into her apartment on the floor below, as well. Plus, the parking garage on the corner offered layer after layer of shadows between each level of concrete. So many hidden areas. So many windows.

Who...?

Her phone beeped with another text.

Green is a lovely color on you.

Laura slowly dropped her focus down to the green-and-gold George Mason University sweatshirt she wore. Oh, hell.

Her lungs constricted with a painful breath. Her pulse thundered in her ears.

He could see her. Right now. Right here. He was watching.

Imaginary laughter rang in her ears as she

bolted for the front door. She fumbled with the lock a moment before stuffing her phone into her back pocket to wipe any prints off the knob. Then she was ducking beneath the yellow tape and pulling the door shut. She stabbed her key into the deadbolt to secure it.

"Taking up a life of crime now, are we?"

She yelped and whirled around to see Conor leaning against the wall across from Chloe's door, his arms folded over the front of his unbuttoned coat.

The cold outside air radiated off him. Or maybe she was going into shock. "How did you know where I was?"

"Um, I'm a detective? And I happen to know you pretty darn well…" She didn't need an explanation or a joke or a reprimand. She needed warmth and strength and an anchor she could hold on to. Without a word or even a conscious breath, she tugged Conor's arms apart, slipped her hands inside the front of his coat and walked straight into his chest. His arms folded around her when she turned her cheek to the steady thump of his heart. "Whoa. My God, you're shaking." His hold on her tightened, pulling her onto her toes. His hand cupped the nape of her neck, his lips brushing the crown of her hair. "Honey, what's wrong?"

Laura needed a few seconds of his clean, cold

scent filling her head, a few seconds of his hard body surrounding hers, a few seconds of the innate caring Conor had always given her, before she could ease the grip she had around his waist and lean back against the cradle of his arms. His blue eyes were so dark, so worried.

"He's watching me. He knew I was in Chloe's apartment." She reached into her back pocket without breaking the contact between them. She'd surely lose it if he ever let her go. She pulled up the texts and handed him the phone, sliding back into the heat beneath his coat, clinging to him with all the strength she had left. "He's watching."

Chapter Eight

The first thing Conor did after securing the dead bolt to Laura's apartment was cross to the living room window and close the blinds. If the killer was spying on her, he intended to make the bastard's efforts to get eyes on Laura as difficult as possible.

The second thing he did was to take her hand and fold it squarely into his palm. She needed the contact to stay calm, feel reassured. And quite frankly, so did he. Together they moved through her apartment, checking locks, closing blinds. The dimness cast a pall over her apartment where the brightness of the winter afternoon had once lit it with the sunlight and color he associated with Laura. Although he regretted casting her life into the shadows, he preferred the seclusion to knowing that the spying creep who'd been calling and texting had any kind of advantage over her.

The third thing he did was shuck out of his coat and sit on her sofa. He adjusted the gun on his hip and pulled Laura down beside him, wrapping her up in his arms when she curled into a ball, tucking her head against his shoulder.

She'd stopped shaking. She didn't cry. She didn't talk. But something about the way her fingers fisted in his sweater and T-shirt, pressing into the skin and muscle underneath, and the way her short legs curled over his lap as if she needed every inch of human contact he could offer, tore at him inside.

Conor had been in protector mode before, knowing Laura was poking her nose into things that were better left to law enforcement to investigate.

But now, after he'd read those damned texts and felt the fear vibrating through her body, adrenaline pumped in him, putting him in amped-up super-protective mode. It was like he was back working WITSEC again, on that last protection assignment he'd run in Kansas City. That was two years ago, when his idiot boss had agreed to leak information about *his* witness in order to use her as bait to make the Badge Man, the serial killer who'd murdered her husband and tried to kill her, reveal himself so he could be captured. His job was to keep people safe from those who wanted them dead. Period. That had been the final straw that had convinced Conor to leave the Marshals Service and go to work at KCPD. Because it was his friends at KCPD who had stepped up to help him keep his witness safe when the killer had shown up to silence the only surviving eyewitness to a serial killer's crimes.

But he wasn't in Kansas City now. He had neither WITSEC resources he could call on, nor a local police force he trusted to back him up with Laura's safety.

And damn if it didn't infuriate every cell in his body to know some wacko out there who'd already murdered her friend was getting his jollies by taunting Laura with threats and making this smart, funny, full-of-life woman afraid. It wasn't just anger simmering in his veins, either. There was a far too familiar ache squeezing at his chest—that ache of knowing he could lose someone who was growing more precious, more necessary to his sanity and emotional well-being with every passing second. He'd already lost so much—he wasn't sure he had the strength to lose anyone else who mattered to him.

So, he damn well wasn't going to let anybody hurt Laura.

He held her for as long as he could before the need to act grew too great, and he had to do something.

When he felt her finally relax against him, Conor tunneled his fingers into the silky waves at the nape of her neck. He started a slow massage, apologizing for the tension he was about to re-kindle there. "Tell me what you found in Chloe's apartment," he whispered at the top of her head. "Because I'm guessing you figured something out and went to check it out all by yourself—and this guy knows, or at least suspects, you found whatever it is he's looking for."

She nodded, then reached into her pocket and pressed a flash drive stick into his palm. "I decoded Chloe's message about the cat." She pointed to the silly red dog on her desk. "She made each of us a statue when she was first experimenting with her animal sculptures. She made me a dog, and herself a blue cat."

"This was inside?"

She nodded, pulling her legs off his lap and drawing a handful of confetti from her pocket. She leaned forward, arranging the strips of paper on the coffee table in front of them. Conor frowned at what he could only label a blackmail note. "This was wrapped around the flash drive. I think these were what she was originally going to send me for safekeeping."

"Until someone showed up unexpectedly, and she knew she had to get rid of it. The cat was her plan B." Conor cursed at whatever horrible thing was on this flash drive. "Why would she get you involved with something like this?"

The Laura he knew was back in her eyes when

she turned to face him. "Because she didn't have anybody else."

Conor brushed aside the caramel lock that had fallen across her forehead and studied the compassion in her green-gold eyes. "Is it your mission in life to be there for every lost soul who crosses your path?"

She pressed her cheek into his lingering hand. "Only the ones I...really care about."

The caring didn't surprise him, but he sensed that she'd been about to say something different. Something specific to him. He knew the feelings between them were changing, intensifying, getting complicated. Was she as reluctant to put a name to those feelings as he was? Did she need the reliability of their relationship to sustain her the way he seemed to need her?

He didn't ask her to elaborate, and he didn't try to explain the complexity of his feelings, either. Instead, she gathered up the shredded note and flash drive and carried them both to her desk. Conor rose and followed her while she booted up her computer.

He sat on the ottoman beside the desk while she took the chair. "Did you receive the package Chloe mailed to you today?"

Laura nodded, still looking a little pale for his liking, but she seemed to be functioning again. She pulled an envelope from the top right drawer and dropped the pieces of paper inside it. "Deputy Cobb was here. He took the letter after I read it. That's all it was. A padded envelope with a letter. But I think initially Chloe had the flash drive in the package. It had been cut open and resealed. Part of the original letter had been crossed out, and she scribbled another message about watching her cat instead. That's when I put two and two together and found this." She nodded to the flash drive on the desk in front of her. "Are you going to turn me in?"

"Are we going to see what's on it?" He reached over to squeeze her hand. When she smiled, something inside him lightened up, too. He picked up the flash drive himself and inserted it into the side of the computer. "Let's see what you found, Nancy Drew."

The icon that popped up was labeled *Vinnie and Me*. Not incriminating in and of itself, but it certainly gave Conor an indication of what to expect when Laura clicked on the icon and the list of files appeared. They were all video and photo files, probably transferred from Chloe's phone, with innocuous names like *Birthday Dinner, First Date, Richmond Art Show, Studio Session 1, 2,* and so on, chronicling her relationship with Vinnie Orlando.

Laura clicked on a couple of the files to discover selfies at restaurants and in front of Washington, DC, landmarks. A few were videos with Chloe's high-pitched voice providing commentary of Vinnie practicing his golf swing at an indoor driving range, or getting the pants beat off him in pool at a local tavern. In that one, Vinnie talked loudly and staggered around the table as if he was drunk, or possibly high. The studio sessions were recordings of works in progress, or snapshots of drawings she wanted to recreate in clay. *Studio Session 5* was apparently Chloe posing nude for Vinnie. She'd filmed him shirtless beside a canvas, painting her while they flirted back and forth. But when she called him over for a selfie together, Laura quickly clicked off the file. "We don't need to look at that, do we?"

She scrolled back up the page where a file name caught Conor's eye. *Ring Shopping.* Curious to follow his hunch, he tapped on the screen. "That one."

He frowned when Laura opened the video and widened it to full screen. That was no mall or jewelry store with bright lights reflecting off display cases full of precious gems and shiny metals. The picture was blurry and dark. He thought he could make out the sounds of breathless panting and a rapid tapping.

"Those are probably Chloe's heels," Laura explained. "I think she's running."

He caught an image of what looked like a wall

of bricks before he heard the slam of several car doors. "Surprise, baby. Mama's early for our naughty date."

"Is that Chloe?" Conor asked, clarifying the source of the woman's voice.

Laura nodded. She tucked her short hair behind her ears and cupped the sides of her neck, giving him a glimpse of the pink staining her cheeks. "Chloe told me that she and Vinnie liked to arrange what she called their 'naughty dates.' They'd have sex in unusual locations. Or, you know, in unusual ways. Looks like they're going for a dark alley here."

For a split second, he was completely sidetracked by the idea of Laura's back flat against a wall with her legs wrapped around his hips. Her cheeks would be flushed with the same heat coursing through him. His name would be on her lips.

Suddenly, his jeans were uncomfortable, and he was hot in ways that had nothing to do with the layers of clothing he wore.

He shouldn't be thinking naughty thoughts about Laura. Only, he couldn't shake the idea that being intimate with Laura felt right, maybe even inevitable. That being with her would be as mind-blowing and as soul-touchingly perfect as her kisses. He wanted her. Her sister had never undermined his control like this. Had there ever been a woman who got under his skin so quickly or distracted him so easily or made him so crazy with the need to touch her that he hadn't even noticed his fingers had traced the same pattern as hers and were now feathered into those silky gold and brown waves behind her ear?

When he saw her eyes were wide and dark and locked onto his, her lips parted in trembling anticipation, he nearly leaned in to cover her mouth with his.

But a hushed whisper from the video turned their attention back to the computer screen.

"Oops." The camera pulled back, as if Chloe had stopped in her tracks. Then the shot turned sideways before righting itself. Now the camera was shooting from a lower angle, with the distinct ridges of a galvanized steel trash can lining the right side of the image, as though Chloe had hunkered down beside the can to remain out of sight of whatever she was filming. "Oh, I don't do that, baby. No friends allowed."

Illumination from a single lamp over a gray steel door indicated Chloe was indeed filming in an alleyway. He could make out the silhouettes of a dumpster and two SUVs or maybe pickup trucks parked beyond the dim circle of light. The steel door sported a logo that included a frothy beer mug and some chipped, unreadable words.

He recognized the sharp nose and brown ponytail of the man pacing in front of the door.

Laura grabbed the mouse and started to click off the video. "That's Vinnie. We probably don't need to see this one, either. For all I know, she filmed the two of them having sex behind a bar."

"Wait." Conor laid his hand over hers when Chloe panned the scene and he saw four other men come into the picture frame from the direction of the vehicles. "Let this play out. I think we're onto something here."

Laura's fingers curled into his and he tightened his grip. "I can't make out the faces on any of those men," she said. "Although those two in the bulky winter coats remind me of Vinnie's entourage. They were with him at Chloe's apartment the other night."

"I remember them." Conor leaned in closer as the two beefy men parted and a shorter, slighter man wearing a longer coat moved between them. "He matches the lawyer Vinnie had with him, Marvin Boltz."

Chloe was talking again, giggling at her own joke. "A suit, a cop and a hottie walk into a bar…"

"A cop?" Laura and Conor echoed together. They both leaned forward to study the fuzzy images.

The fourth man walked up beside the man they suspected could be Boltz. Although the brim of his hat matched the local deputy's uniform, it also kept his face shaded and unrecognizable. The bulky man with the hat nodded at something the could-be-Boltz said. Then he turned to Vinnie, and the light caught the shiny flash of a badge on his chest just before he shoved Vinnie up against the wall, pinning him there.

Laura sat back in her chair. "That looks like Cobb."

"Not enough to prove anything." Not in a court of law, at any rate. But Conor was more and more certain that they'd identified the players in this back-alley meeting.

Chloe's phone camera was too far away to record any of the men's conversation, but she continued her whispered commentary. "What the…? Oh, no, you don't." The man with the badge grabbed Vinnie's ponytail and gave it a hard tug, knocking Vinnie's head against the bricks. "No police brutality without a witness."

Chloe must have thought Vinnie was getting roughed up by the cops and wanted to film evidence of it. But this was something else. She realized it, too, when Vinnie put his hands up in surrender and the man with the badge backed off. Vinnie reached inside his jacket and pulled out a small plastic bag filled with white powder. "Oh, baby. Don't put that stuff in your body."

The man in the suit smacked the drugs out of

Vinnie's hand. Vinnie protested while the smaller man lectured him, slapping him a few times about the face. Then the smaller man straightened the front of Vinnie's jacket and stepped back. Whatever he'd said had finally silenced Vinnie into submission. While the man with the badge picked up the bag of drugs, Vinnie walked to the car parked closest to Chloe. Some of the picture disappeared as she retreated farther into her hiding place. But because she was closer, when she panned to the rear of the car, Conor could make out the red color. And a partial license plate number.

Conor turned to Laura. "Do you have pen and paper?"

But she was already writing down the numbers. "Something, something, two, four, zero, nine. That looks like Vinnie's car."

The men followed Vinnie to the back of the car where he popped open the trunk. The men were close enough to make out a few words now.

"I thought she was asleep," Vinnie said. "She must have already taken something else before we lit up."

"You were right to call me." The slighter man with the long coat shook his head. "Don't say a word about this to anyone. We'll take care of it."

"Her name is—" Vinnie began.

"Names don't matter. Rico? Hammer?" The

older man waved the two thugs over to join them. "Let's get it out of here."

Conor had a really bad feeling about what they were going to see next. But Laura slid him a sideways glance, and he knew any request to let him watch the rest of this video alone wasn't going to happen.

"I know what you're thinking, Wildman," Laura whispered, turning her focus to the monitor. "I want to know why Chloe was killed."

"Okay, Squirt. We'll do this together." Conor tightened his hand around hers and they continued to watch.

Vinnie reached into the trunk and scooped up something lumpy and cylindrical in shape that hung over the ends of his arms. Chloe's whispered commentary started up again. "Is that a…?" A shock of long blond hair tumbled out one end of the bundle. "That's a woman."

Laura gasped right along with Chloe. "A dead woman."

"Wait." The man in the long coat picked up the limp arm that fell from the bundle. He tugged on the dead woman's hand before holding up a small circle of gold that gleamed in the dim light. He smacked Vinnie's cheek. "Are you kidding me with this?"

Laura leaned closer. "That's a ring. The ring Vinnie was looking for?"

Conor nodded. "Something that distinctive could certainly link Vinnie to a crime scene."

Slipping the piece of jewelry into his coat pocket, the older man nodded to the two thuggish men. They took the limp body out of Vinnie's arms and carried it off into the shadows. A few seconds later, a trunk slammed shut. "OMG, seriously? I ride in that car." Chloe's voice got slightly louder as the men walked Vinnie to the back door of the bar. Their voices were beyond hearing again. "Why do you have a dead body? What have you done, baby?"

The guy in the suit patted Vinnie on the back, pointed at him, and said one last thing that made Vinnie shrug off his touch. Then Suit Guy and the man wearing the badge got into their vehicles and drove away. Once he was alone, Vinnie kicked a trash can before stomping back inside the bar.

Chloe pulled back into nearly complete darkness, still recording even though there was no picture. "Something very bad just happened. Does Mommy know about this? I'm guessing she wouldn't be pleased." She laughed. "And she said *I* was the bad influence. I never did drugs a day in my life, but you… Oh, this is too sweet. You know I love you, baby. And I know you love me. This is our chance to be together without Mommy objecting. Trust me, okay?"

She turned the camera to her and Conor

glimpsed the beautiful, animated blonde Chloe had been before her murder. "I just figured out how to get Vinnie to pop the question." She wiggled her bare fingers in front of the camera. "I'm going to finally get my ring. Not that old gold filigree thing she was wearing, but one with a real diamond."

The video ended with a startling blackness.

Laura hugged her arms around her middle. "That's why she was killed. Drugs? A dead woman?" She looked over at Conor. "Chloe thought it was a good idea to show that to somebody? She was in trouble as soon as she recorded it, wasn't she?"

Conor's fingers went to Laura's hair again, to soothe the concern lining her eyes as well as to ease the tension in him with the gentle tickle of the waves tangling with his fingertips. "She played a dangerous gamble, forcing Vinnie to commit to her. I'm sorry she lost. I'm sorry she got you involved."

"If only she would have thought it through. She should have known any one of the men on that video would want to destroy it and anyone who knew..." Laura's eyes lit with an idea. She pointed at the black screen on the monitor. "Who's Mommy?"

"Sounded like Vinnie's mother didn't approve of his relationship with Chloe." Conor reached for the mouse to close the video file. Laura rolled her chair to the side to give him room to pull up the internet and log in to his email. He typed in an address in Kansas City, along with a brief message, attached the video and hit Send. "That could have been her plan—showing the recording to his mother if Vinnie didn't agree to marry her."

Laura sprang from her chair and paced the room. "Chloe was a good person. *Mommy* shouldn't approve of his son buying or selling drugs and hauling around dead bodies. Do you think he killed that woman in the trunk? Or she overdosed while doing drugs with him? Chloe would never be involved with something like that. Her whole life was tainted by her mother's drug use and crimes. She always avoided getting involved with anyone in that lifestyle."

"Her mother said she got greedy." Conor pulled out the flash drive and walked into the kitchen, asking Laura for a plastic bag and pen to label it. The data stick already had their prints on it, jeopardizing its usefulness as evidence, but if there was any chance they could use it to find Chloe's killer and get Laura out of this mess, he was going to take it. "If a guy had enough money, would she overlook his addiction? Or think she could change him? Save him?"

Laura shrugged. "If she really was in love with Vinnie, I could see her believing that marriage would give him stability. If he has issues with his mother, she might think bonding together would make them a team—make them stronger together—to face his mother, or hers, or whatever problems they had to deal with."

"Blackmail isn't a great basis for a lasting relationship."

Laura's eyes tilted up to his. "But it makes sense. If you thought a certain woman was the one—that she was your soul mate like Chloe must have thought about Vinnie—wouldn't you do anything to be together? To stay together? Love makes people hold on to hopes that maybe they shouldn't. Real love makes them fight for what they want. She was fighting to get her man."

Conor instantly thought of Lisa. He'd loved her enough to propose. But like Laura had explained Lisa's feelings at the wedding reception, maybe he hadn't been *in* love with her, after all. He'd settled for the easy comfort of their relationship, the lifetime of expectation that they would one day be together. If he truly believed Lisa was the only woman for him, wouldn't he have fought harder to make their engagement work? He could have changed his job. He could have stayed in Virginia. Although, he could see now that changing who he was to please her wasn't a healthy compromise—not in the long run. Lisa was right—they wouldn't have been happy together. But he'd been broken by the thought of someone leaving him again. His perception of his real feelings might have been clouded by the helplessness he was going through with his mother's illness. But once he'd started to heal from that loss, he would have said or done something more if he truly believed she was the only woman for him. Instead, he'd let her go without a fight.

He watched Laura as she put away the leftovers from her lunch and cleaned the kitchen. Seeing her do those simple tasks or tuck her hair behind her ear or touch his arm when she needed him to step aside so she could return the box of sandwich bags to its drawer hit him like a sucker punch to the gut. Even without the fancy pink dress showcasing her every curve, she was a pretty, sexy woman. He felt a sort of possessive caveman awareness heat his blood when she came close enough for him to inhale that subtly exotic scent that was all Laura.

The admission was telling. He felt more compelled to bend the rules—to strap on his gun and protect Laura, to hunt down the men in that video and put them out of commission so they could never threaten her again—than he ever had been motivated to fight for anything in the years he'd been with Lisa. He wasn't just fighting for Laura's safety, or perhaps fighting for her life—he was fighting for whatever this was that was happening between them.

Yeah. He understood what had driven Chloe Wilson to use that incriminating video to ensure she could be with the man she loved.

Because he was in love with Laura.

This wasn't any rebound from losing her sister. She wasn't any second-best consolation prize. This felt like… He wasn't sure what this felt like because he'd never had feelings this intense before. He'd been waiting for the right woman, the one who got him and accepted him the way he was, the one he'd always shared a special bond with, to grow up. She had.

Now what was he going to do about it?

"Conor?" He realized she'd said something. That he'd been staring long and hard at her without really listening to what she was saying. He snapped himself out of his head and brought his focus back to the conversation. "Are you going to turn the flash drive over to Deputy Cobb? Is that what you're trying to decide?"

"No." He pushed away from the counter he'd been leaning against and crossed into the living room where he stashed the makeshift evidence bag in the pocket of his coat. "He doesn't get his hands on this. For one thing, I don't want you implicated in any kind of illegal seizure of evidence. And two, I don't trust him. If there's any chance the cop in that video is him, then he already knows too much about you. That's why he's doing such a lousy job investigating the murder. He's stalling, buying time to find this before he gets implicated."

She followed him out to the living room. "Could he have killed Chloe?"

"It's possible. Or one of the other men in that video. Even Vinnie himself."

"Or Mommy?"

Conor nodded. "I don't think we should trust anybody local for now. Let me call a friend of mine in Kansas City, a retired detective and consultant with KCPD. I emailed him a copy of this video and asked him to look up some information. He can run the partial license plate. I'll see if he can track down who Vinnie's mother is and run a background check on Cobb. One of his sons works at the crime lab there. Maybe Niall can call in a favor and see if a tech can clean up the video, so we can identify the other men and who that woman might be. Confirm that it's Boltz and Cobb, or, clear them as suspects."

"Your friend and his family would do all that for you? For me?" She nodded, seeing the affirmative answer written on his face. "No wonder you have such strong ties to Kansas City. You didn't have that kind of support here."

"If Thomas Watson can help us, he will. He's

married to a former witness of mine. I was her man of honor when they got married in front of a judge there in KC. It's a little complicated, but if Cobb is involved in this, Thomas will definitely help us. He has a particular dislike for dirty cops." That was a story for another time.

"If he's that much of a straight arrow, won't he want to arrest me for taking that flash drive from Chloe's apartment?"

"Not if I explain the circumstances and put in a good word for you. And I will."

"Thank you. For being here when I need you." She braced her hand against his chest and stretched up on tiptoe, curling her fingers behind his neck to bring his mouth down for a kiss. "For everything."

He didn't need any encouragement to open his mouth over hers and drink in the gift she offered. His hands settled at her hips, sliding beneath the hem of her sweatshirt to find warm skin at the nip of her waist. She slipped her arms around his neck, pulling her shorter frame as tall as it could go to keep her lips aligned beneath his, softly pulling at him, demanding more pressure here, a tiny stroke of his tongue there. Conor answered every request, giving, taking, and giving more until she whimpered that needy hum of desire in her throat. The sexy sound demanded his attention there and he lowered his head to chase the husky vibration along the arch of her neck. Her skin was sweet and smooth beneath his lips, warming at every touch.

Oh, yeah. This was one hell of a thank-you. Although, exactly who was being grateful for what got lost in the passion arcing between them. He just knew he had to touch her, taste her, to believe that she wanted him as badly as he wanted her.

Laura threw her head back, offering him the chance to taste the indentation at the base of her throat, encouraging him to push aside the neckline of her sweatshirt and nip at the juncture of her neck and shoulder. Her fingertips dug into his shoulders, seeking purchase as she squirmed against him. With her hips bumping against his zipper, he couldn't exactly hide the effect she was having on him. She moaned in frustration before grabbing either side of his face and pulling his mouth back to hers. Her fingers skimmed through his hair and cupped his scalp, holding his lips against hers while he licked and teased and plundered, giving back the same and more—taking charge of the kiss one moment, submitting to his driving need the next, then meeting him somewhere in the middle—until muscles weakened and gravity kicked in. Her toes slid back to the floor, easing the ferocity of the kiss.

Conor spread his legs to make himself shorter, but it was proving equally frustrating for him to have their mouths mesh so perfectly, when their bodies felt like two mismatched puzzle pieces struggling to find a way to fit. Switching tactics, she dropped her hands to his waist, lifting his sweater and tugging at his shirt. When her fingertips brushed against the skin above his belt buckle, he hissed at the jolt of awareness that arrowed through him. Her hands brushed against his holster anchored to his belt. For a moment, he remembered how Lisa had always wanted him to remove his weapon before she touched him, even casually, as if she feared it more than she'd ever wanted him. But that memory and the momentary pang of doubt vanished like popping bubbles when Laura dug her fingertips into the sensitive skin at his spine, and her lips scudded across his jaw and took a playful bite of his chin. There was no hesitation in how she touched him. She wanted to feel skin, muscle, heat.

There was no hesitation to her kisses, either. She swirled her tongue inside his mouth, whispered his name against his lips and pulled her body into his. He went nearly mindless as the thrusting tips of her lush breasts branded him through the layers of clothing they wore. He needed more. He needed her. She wanted contact. So did he.

"Arms around my neck," he ordered, gentling the command with a kiss.

When she shifted her grip on him, Conor tightened his arms around her. He palmed her sweet round rump and lifted Laura off the floor, taking all her weight as she fell against him, flattening all those curves against the hard need of his body. Heat matched heat as her legs wrapped around him, infusing him with a strength that made it easy to hold her against him with one hand. The other snuck beneath her shirt again, palming the straight line of her back, sliding around to capture the heavy weight of her breast through its satin and lace casing. When he caught the pearled nipple between his hand and thumb, Laura gasped into his mouth. Then she rested her forehead against his neck, proudly pushing the eager flesh into his hand even as she sighed with pleasure against his skin.

"Are we really doing this?" she whispered.

That was his intention. Conor was gauging the shorter distance to the sofa or kitchen counter where he could set her down and get more of these clothes out of the way when his phone rang.

Conor swore. He kissed her again, apologizing for the foul word so close to her lips. "I'm sorry, honey." His back pocket rang again. "It startled me."

"It's okay." She straightened her legs, eased her grip on his shoulders, and his body felt a chill at the loss of her wrapped around him. "Reality sucks, huh? Maybe we should think about this, anyway."

"Maybe we should." Was that what she wanted? What did he want?

Ring.

Her lips were rosy and swollen with the stamp of his lips, the delicate skin around her mouth abraded with the scratch of his beard stubble. Her eyes looked as dazed as he felt when she looked up at him. "You are one hell of a good kisser, Conor Wildman."

Her smile felt like a reward, and Conor was eager to earn as many of those as he could. "So are you."

She was standing on her own two feet when it rang a fourth time. "You'd better get that."

He pulled the phone from his pocket. Thomas Watson's name flashed on the screen. "I do need to take this," Conor apologized, planting one last kiss on Laura's lips.

She reached up to smooth the hair she'd raked out of place before backing away. Was she okay? Had he gone too far? Had he not gone far enough? She pointed to his phone when it rang again. "He's your friend in Kansas City?" He nodded. "Would you like some coffee while you talk to him?"

"Yeah. Coffee would be good." Or a stiff drink. Or getting his head examined.

While she walked into the kitchen, he answered Thomas's call. "Wildman. Thanks for getting back—"

"What the hell do you mean sending me something like that, and then not answering your damn phone?" Thomas's tone was a mix of joking and concern. "You're supposed to be on vacation, visiting your old hometown. What kind of trouble have you gotten yourself into?"

Thomas had more connections and wisdom about the job than any detective Conor knew. If anyone could get the answers he needed without raising a red flag that would jeopardize Laura's safety here in Virginia, Thomas could.

He strode across the living room. Sitting was out of the question for the moment, until he got getting Laura naked off his mind and got his head back in the detective game. "We have to work on your timing, Thomas."

Sometime later, Conor was jotting notes at Laura's desk and wrapping up the conversation with Thomas when she sat on the leather ottoman beside him. She'd given up pretending to read a magazine over on the couch. She'd been hanging on to his every word, and now she was craning her neck around his shoulder to see his scribbles on the notepad. Grinning at her ceaseless curiosity, he scooted the pad in front of her, so she could read the information Thomas had been able to find out already.

Laura's phone? Different call/text number each time. Disposable cells? Pro.

Identity of dead woman? Running missing persons search.

Chloe Wilson—death listed as suspicious, under investigation, Arlington County sheriff's department. No other info. Short-staffed? Incompetence? Cover-up?

Vinnie—extensive record: petty crimes, drugs, court-ordered rehab/no hard time.

Father deceased. No record of mother's death. Remarried? No Mona Orlando in VA or DC area. "Mommy"?

Conor let her decode the information for herself while he shared some of his suspicions with Thomas. "I don't know if Vinnie comes from organized crime or old money or what—but keeping this video out of *Mommy's* hands seems to be the key to the blackmail. Orlando's got an attorney named Marvin Boltz. Maybe he actually works for *Mommy* and is keeping an eye on Vinnie for her."

"Marvin Boltz." Thomas's deep, patient voice repeated the name as he took down the information. "I'll call you as soon as I find out anything else."

"Anything you can tell me about Cobb is priority one. I need to know who I can trust around here."

"Got it. Conor?"

"Yes, sir?" He heard the paternal warning in Thomas's tone, and felt heartened by it, rather than defensive. His own father hadn't been around to tell him when he was doing something stupid or dangerous. And though Thomas wasn't going to change Conor's mind on this plan of action, he appreciated that the older man cared enough to remind him of the risk he was taking.

"You're off the books with this one—interviewing suspects on a case that isn't yours? Not reporting the stalking incidents to the local authorities? Stealing evidence from a crime scene?"

"Technically, it wasn't stealing. Laura had a key. The victim directed her to take possession of it."

He could imagine Thomas shaking his head. "You won't win that argument in front of a judge."

"I don't have to. I just need enough intel to identify where the threat is coming from, so I can protect Laura. It'll be somebody else's case to prosecute."

"What about interfering with another jurisdiction's investigation? Even if your deputy is part of this, not every cop on the force there is. They won't appreciate you taking down one of their own or giving them any bad press. Is this woman worth your career?"

Conor bumped Laura's shoulder with his to get her to look up at him. He smiled. "Yes."

"Hopefully, it won't come to that. Be careful. I've gotten used to having you around."

"Yes, sir. I'll see you in a few days."

"You'd better."

Laura's eyes narrowed with unspoken questions as he ended the call. She knew he'd been talking about her but couldn't figure out what he'd admitted to Thomas. He still needed some time to adjust to the idea himself, and then decide how he was going to deal with it. He didn't have a good track record with relationships. And though Laura had made it clear enough that she was attracted to him, too, and knew she cared about him on some level, did he want to risk losing what they had by pushing for something more? Could they be happy enough in the short term that if it didn't work out, he'd be left with a good memory instead of the soul-rotting guilt that he'd destroyed their friendship?

"What?"

Conor had to look away from the question in those sweet hazel eyes. He didn't know the answer himself yet.

Since he wasn't forthcoming, she picked up their coffee mugs and returned to the kitchen.

"You think that was Cobb in the video, too, don't you. This morning, he acted like he expected to find more than that letter inside the package. Do you think he knows about the flash drive? Could he be the one calling and texting me?"

Right. The investigation was a lot easier to talk about than his feelings, or where that kiss had been leading, so Conor tucked the notes inside his pocket and followed her. "It's a logical deduction even for Cobb to make. It explains why Chloe's computer and phone were taken. The killer was looking for the video."

"He gives me the creeps." She loaded the mugs into the dishwasher before turning off the coffee maker. They'd probably drunk enough coffee today to keep them awake for three more days. But fighting their mutual caffeine addiction wasn't the reason she'd paused with the half-full pot over the sink. "Downstairs at the mailbox, he grabbed me when my thoughts wandered off—"

"Did he hurt you?" Conor was at her side in an instant, wanting to read the truth in her eyes, hating the idea of the deputy's beefy hands on Laura's perfect, petite body.

"No." She inhaled a deep breath of the toasty, rich brew before dumping it down the sink. "He smells bad, though. Way too much cologne. I don't know any woman who thinks that's sexy. Maybe he knows his charm's no good and he's overcompensating." He grinned at that. Good. She was making a joke. Cobb hadn't scared her too much. But something had. And he didn't think it was that kiss. "Speaking of cologne…" Her gaze lingered at the middle of his chest before she tilted her eyes to his. "I think someone was in my apartment last night. After we left the cemetery. While we were at Mom and Dad's eating dinner."

"When were you going to tell me that?" She'd had a break-in, and was just now mentioning it? "With everything that's been going on the past few days, you didn't think to lead any one of our conversations today with that bit of news?"

She raised her hands, patting his chest like he was her nephew who could be appeased with a toy truck, trying to soothe the concern that had sparked his temper. "The clues were there—I just didn't see it. Nothing's been taken. There were a few things rearranged in my desk. I thought I was brain-dead from a lack of sleep, and that I'd imagined it. I smelled something foreign in here earlier, too." She pulled her hands away to hug her arms around her waist. "They searched my apartment, didn't they?"

Hell. Even if it was a "There, there, baby boy" pat, he craved that contact with her if only to reassure himself that she was okay. Conor reached for her. "I told you to call me if anything seemed hinky to you."

She swatted his hand away and retreated from him. "*Everything* seems hinky to me now."

"I need you to look again. Are you sure nothing is missing?"

"There wasn't anything to take." She hurried into the living room and brushed her hand across his coat, where he'd put the flash drive. "I didn't have that video until just before you got here. If they searched, they didn't find anything."

He was scaring her, making her run from him. Conor planted his feet on the rug and let her pace. He inhaled a deep breath, cooling his tone if not his suspicion. "You don't have a landline, do you?"

She shook her head.

"Maybe they came in to bug your phone. When that didn't work, they left." When she moved closer to the door, he went to the window to peek through the blinds and survey the vehicles on the street below, and all the windows across the street with easy access to view her apartment. "Have you seen anyone outside, watching the building?"

She waited a beat too long for him to know he wasn't going to like her answer. "Only Deputy Cobb. But he was waiting for the envelope. He hasn't been back since…"

Her skin went pale beneath her freckles, and

the dimple of that worry frown reappeared on her forehead. Conor reached her in three long strides. "What is it?"

She reached into the back pocket of her jeans. "My phone just vibrated with another text. I'm afraid to read it." She swiped the photo off the lock screen and flinched. "It's his number."

When she tried to hand the phone off to him, he caught her hand before she could let go. "I'm right here, honey. We need to see what it says."

She punched the button to open the text, then quickly wrapped her arms around his waist and read it from the corner of her eye. As if a sideways glance could lessen the impact of the threat Conor held in his hand.

You can't hide from me, Laura. I know you found it. You just signed your death warrant. At first, all I wanted was that flash drive. But now I'm coming for you.
There's no place you can hide.
Not even your boyfriend can save you now.

Conor swore. Forget keeping his distance. Whoever was behind this had all the advantages. He needed to change the odds into Laura's favor. He stuffed her phone into his own pocket and tugged on her hand, pulling her down the hallway to her bedroom. "Pack a bag. You're coming with me."

She opened her mouth to protest.

"I'm not asking." He opened her closet door and found her suitcase. He tossed it onto the bed. "You got anything smaller?"

She nudged him aside to unzip the suitcase and pull out a matching overnight bag. "Where am I going? How long am I going to be gone?"

"Mom's house for now. As long as it takes. My old bedroom is still set up for when I visit. I can sleep on the couch."

"I'm couch-sized. I'll sleep there," she offered. Her hands were shaking as she packed clothes and toiletries. "Even if I gave them that flash drive now, they'd want to kill me because I've watched it. I'm connected to Chloe. They have no idea how much she told me. I'm a loose end." She pulled a pair of boots out of her closet to add to the bag. "Is it wrong to wish Isaac had lost his temper and hurt her? That she was a victim of domestic violence and not…" She spun to face him. "Am I going to be another dead woman in a trunk somewhere?"

"I won't let them hurt you." Conor tunneled his fingers into her hair and tilted her face up to his. "I'm with you 24/7 now."

"Until you leave town again. What if the cops never catch those men? What do I do then?"

Her lack of faith in him hurt worse than any abandonment he'd felt with Lisa or his father. "I'm not leaving until this is solved. Until I know you're safe. You're too important to me to allow anyone to hurt you."

She evaluated his promise for several seconds before she nodded. "I wish you'd stopped at 'I'm not leaving.'" She pulled away to zip the bag shut. "Let's go."

Chapter Nine

"I told you I'd sleep on the couch."

Conor tossed a T-shirt into his black leather bag and tried not to make too much of Laura sitting on the edge of the bed where he'd slept the night before. "Hardly seems gentlemanly."

"Since when were you a gentleman?"

He grinned at the teasing remark, tucking the plastic bag holding the flash drive that had caused all this trouble safely into one of the zippered pockets. "I can be if I try."

"Don't knock yourself out on my account."

Was this just one of their usual tongue-in-cheek exchanges? Or was she hinting that she'd be okay if he stayed right here in the bed with her? She wasn't making it easy to be a stand-up guy and do the right thing. And he was determined to do the right thing by Laura, no matter what happened over the next few days or hours or however long they had to be together like this.

His body hummed with awareness of the tension underlying the playful banter. "Sounds like it might be safer out in the other room."

"Safer for whom?"

He laughed out loud at that taunt, mostly because pushing her down on the mattress and finishing what they'd started earlier at her apartment was the only other option he could think of at the moment. His laughter quickly faded, though, when she didn't join in.

The cheeseburgers, fries and sodas they'd gotten on the way here, plus the extra distance from her apartment and the chance to explain the situation to her parents and arrange for them to take some precautions had gone a long way to restore Laura's spirit, if not her cheerful outlook on her immediate future. He retrieved his toiletry kit from the adjoining bathroom and added them to the bag, too. His suit, tie and dress shoes could stay in the closet. He wouldn't need them for sleeping or for running, should her texting tormentor make good on his vow to silence her, and a quick escape proved necessary.

"I'm not too sure your father was thrilled to learn how involved I've gotten with his youngest daughter. He seems to think that you should still be playing up in that tree house, not sleeping with a grown man in a house that has only one bed. We may have talked them into leaving town for a few days, but a dad's a dad." Next, he added the spare ammunition boxes for both his service Glock and the Beretta strapped to his ankle. "When they get home, I'd like to at least be able to tell him that I tried to keep my distance."

She got up and turned away from him as soon as the hardware came out, feigning a sudden interest in exploring the bedroom that had been his before he'd gone off to college and gotten his own place. "Dad likes you."

"As a family friend—not as the guy puttin' the moves on his baby girl." He zipped the bag shut. "Besides, I prefer to be between you and the front door, if somebody tries to break in."

And there the joking ended.

Her back stiffened before she reached out to touch the double-globed lamp painted with ornate greenery and daffodils. The smile she turned to give him didn't reach her eyes. "I remember this. Your mom and mine took a china painting class together one summer."

"I think every room in the house had a hand-painted lamp as a result. That's the only one that survived." He extended his arms out to either side, trying to keep the mood light for her. "You know, teenage boys with long, gangly limbs they can't always control?"

Finally. There was the real smile he wanted to see. "You broke all of them?"

"Except for that one. Mom changed her lighting choices to brass and wrought iron after that. It improved their chances of survival."

Laura's laugh was worth a thousand smiles.

But his victory didn't last.

She came back to the bed to pick up his bag, testing the weight of it before setting it back down on the quilt. "Do you always travel with your own personal arsenal?"

"Usually, I keep it in the car with my Kevlar and other duty gear." He tried to read the expression in her eyes. "Does it scare you?"

"Yes. There's a lot of killing power in there and on you. But you know how to use it, right? It's part of your job? I have a feeling you've had training I can't even imagine."

"It's called a go bag. It includes a little of everything we might need if we have to leave in a hurry or we get stranded somewhere, complete with disposable cell phones, a first aid kit and protein bars if we don't have access to food." He'd already turned off her cell phone and removed the battery, so that bastard couldn't call or text her again. He'd replaced it with a disposable cell, had her program in his and Thomas Watson's number, and had her tell her boss that she'd miss a few days of work due to a family emergency. If anyone else called, he'd instructed her not to answer. "We'll lighten up the bag you brought here, pare it down to the essentials, just like mine."

"Minus the weaponry."

"Have you had firearms training?" She shook her head. "Then all you're carrying is some spare ammo." Since the doubt in her eyes wasn't going away, he unsnapped his holster and pulled out his Glock. "I'd better show you this."

"I'm just carrying the ammunition, right?"

"This is more for your safety than the expectation that you'll have to use it. These aren't toys—they're built to kill. I don't want any accidents."

He hated that he had to have this conversation with her about guns, but he appreciated that she didn't shy away from it. He put the Glock into her hands so she could feel the weight of it, reminding her to keep it pointed down and away, and showed her the key parts. "This one doesn't have a separate safety to disengage. Just pulling back on the trigger half a click unlocks it. Don't go anywhere near that trigger unless you're ready to use it."

Holding it the way he'd taught her, she quickly handed it back. "I won't."

He showed her the Beretta, as well, pointing out the thumb safety on the stock, and warning her about the different rounds for each gun not being interchangeable. She seemed less afraid of the lighter weapon but was just as eager to return it.

"Have I scared you out of trusting me yet?"

"No. You're Conor."

Just being Conor Wildman hadn't always been enough. But if it was enough for Laura, then he was going to try to let go of those old insecurities and be the man she needed.

"If at any time I feel I can't handle your protection detail myself, we'll head to Kansas City, where I know I've got backup I can count on. We'd be far enough out of Cobb's jurisdiction that he shouldn't be able to track us. We'd have time and space there to figure this all out and bring Chloe's killer to justice. I didn't give Cobb the address for Mom's house, but if he figures out you're with me, and he grows a few brain cells about how to do police work, he might be able to trace you here. The go bags are just a precaution. Changing locations frequently keeps us off anybody's radar." He carried his bag out to the living room and put it at the foot of the sofa where Laura picked up the sheets and blanket he'd set out and started making up a place to sleep for him. Conor grabbed the opposite end of the sheet to tuck it around the cushions. "Lisa never liked it that I knew this stuff. But I know how to hide. I know how to run. I know how to lie with a straight face, and I know how to fight. I will use every one of those skills to keep you safe from whoever the hell is behind this. You listen to me and do what I tell you. I make no guarantees that anything about this will be easy. But I will get you through this. I promise."

Laura fluffed up his pillow and set it against the arm of the sofa before she faced him. She laid her hand at the center of his chest, splaying her fingers to rest them over his heart. "I'm glad you know those things."

His heart seemed to beat harder, trying to reach out to meet her gentle touch. He couldn't remember a time when he hadn't craved even that most simple of contact with her. Stepping into the press of her hand, he tunneled his fingers into her hair, cradled her head back into his palms and lowered his mouth to kiss her.

The sparks he felt at that first soft touch of her lips kindled a fire in his blood. Her fingers tightened in the front of his sweater. Her lips parted in the ready welcome he was becoming addicted to. The kiss was languid and reassuring and necessarily brief. The hour was late and there were still a few details they needed to sort out.

Conor rested his forehead against Laura's and breathed deeply, committing her scent to memory, counting the freckles that dusted her cheeks, allowing the heat arcing between them to slowly dissipate.

Then he pulled her arm around the back of his waist and walked her to the bedroom. "All right. Some basic rules. Stay inside. Stay away from the windows. If we do have to move out quickly, stay close to my side. Always let me enter or leave a room first. No calling anyone unless I approve it. No getting online. If I say run, you book it as fast as those little legs of yours can go. If I say down, you dive for the ground."

"Anything else?" she tried to joke. "Need me to stand on my head if you clap three times or whistle Dixie if you snore?"

He hugged her to his side and kissed the crown of her hair before releasing her. "My rules should do just fine."

She nodded as she circled the bed and pulled back the covers. She sat on the edge of the bed to untie the ankle boots she wore. They'd already agreed to sleep in their clothes instead of changing into pajamas, again to make a quick escape if necessary. She dropped the first boot to the floor and paused. "Do you think my family understands you sending them away?"

"They understand that it's easier for me to protect one person than a bunch of you."

"Couldn't Vinnie or Cobb go after them in an effort to flush me out?"

Conor leaned his shoulder against the doorframe. "Only as a last resort. These men are looking to do damage control and make their problem go away. Killing an entire family is hardly going to keep them off front page news."

"Killing?"

Damn it, he was scaring her again. "I'm not saying it's impossible, but if Ron and Leslie follow my instructions and avoid using their credit cards, they'll be hard to track. Lisa and Joe are already in the Caribbean on their honeymoon. And Tim can use his legal connections to keep Linda and their sons safe."

"Chloe played a dangerous game and it backfired on her. Now it could backfire on all of us." Laura stood. "Even you. You saw that video, too. If you hadn't tried to help me—"

"I've been a survivor all my life. I don't intend to change that now." He straightened away from the door, needing to get back to that couch before he couldn't walk away anymore. "You look like you're about to drop. Get some sleep. It's been a long day."

"It's been a long weekend."

"Good night, Laura."

She looked small and vulnerable as she nodded and sat to remove the other boot. "Good night, Conor."

Ignoring the way his arms itched to hold her, pretending there wasn't something sharp and painful twisting inside him that wanted to do whatever was necessary to make her smile again, he pulled the door shut. He'd already covered all the windows and checked the locks, but he made one more security sweep through the two-story house before returning to the living room and stripping down to his T-shirt and jeans. He unhooked the ankle holster and tucked the Beretta into his bag before sliding beneath the blanket on the couch. He left his holster on his belt but set his Glock within easy reach on the floor beside him. Then he turned off the lamp and closed his eyes.

They popped open just a few minutes later when he heard a low-pitched whimper in the darkness. Conor knew the house well enough to instantly identify where the sound had come from. A sniffle, as quiet as the soft mewling that had alerted him, turned his head toward his old bedroom. Crying. His mother had cried once, toward the end of her stay in hospice, when she realized she wouldn't be seeing her grandchildren. There wasn't a sound in the world that could twist his insides into a harder knot.

He hadn't been able to do anything to help his mother beyond holding her hand and sharing his handkerchief. There hadn't been any promises he could make that could add time to her life or give her those grandbabies.

Laura was crying.

Sleep wasn't an option now. Not if she was sad or hurting or afraid.

Conor holstered his weapon before padding softly across the cool wood floor. He knocked on the door before pushing it open. With the shades drawn and the lights off, he could barely make out her shape in the bed. But the tears were legit, and each sob she fought to suppress, each sniffle that escaped, tore at him. "You okay, Squirt?"

He heard a rustling beneath the covers and saw the silhouette of her sitting up. "Did I wake you?" He heard the distinct sound of a tissue being used. "I'm sorry."

He crossed to the bedside table and turned on the lamp his mother had painted. He plucked a couple more tissues from the box beside the bed and handed them to Laura as he sat on the edge of the bed, facing her. "You didn't answer my question." She dabbed at her nose and eyes and wiped the trails of tears off her cheeks. "You're not okay."

She tossed the used tissues onto the table and rolled her red-rimmed eyes heavenward before meeting his worried gaze. "I'm having a weak moment."

"I think you're entitled." Her hair was tousled and sexy, and neither the quilt that covered her lap nor the thick-knit sweater she wore could mask the siren call of her curves. But all he could see was the bleak despair in her puffy eyes. "If you need a good cry, go for it."

But now her sadness was tinged with anger.

She fisted the tissue in her lap and shook it. "Why couldn't I leave things well enough alone?"

"You wanted to help your friend."

"I should have just called the police and let them handle Chloe's murder."

Conor took her hand, prying the defenseless tissue from her grasp and warming her stiff fingers against his jeans. "You *did* call the police. Me."

"I got you involved in this when all you wanted was to come for the wedding and get back to Missouri. I feel like I'm forcing you to stay with me. I put you in terrible danger. I put everyone in terrible danger." She shifted her grip and grabbed on to his hand with both of hers. "Two women are already dead. I keep imagining all the horrible things that could happen to me, or my family—or you."

Conor shrugged and tried to elicit a smile. "I'm Conor Wildman. Rebel bad boy next door. Nothing's going to happen to me."

At that, Laura pushed the covers back and sat up on her knees, making herself taller, putting her body closer to his. She wasn't laughing. "Then you're a bad boy with a heart of gold. You're the best friend I've ever had. And I..." She paused to summon her courage. Her eyes glowed with golden flecks of emotion in the dim light from the lamp. "I'm guessing this isn't what you want to hear, but, in case something happens, and I can't say it later, I love you."

"I love you, too, Squirt."

"No." She shook her head and scooted closer until her knee touched his thigh. "I am *in* love with you. I have been for as long as I can remember. Of course, when I was younger, I didn't understand what I was feeling. And then you were with Lisa, and I wanted you both to be happy, so I ignored those feelings. Even when you two were struggling, I was willing to stand aside because you wanted that relationship to work, and I wanted you both to be happy. You never saw me as anything other than her kid sister, anyway."

Love? While his heart leaped at the idea of Laura thinking she was in love with him, the wiser, self-preserving, world-weary logic in him put up an invisible warning hand. He'd accept her caring and her kisses any day of the week, but he wasn't going to set himself up for any more pain. It hurt when he grinned this time, but he did it. "Hey, I'm back up on that pedestal. I'm a girl's teenage crush again."

"Don't make a joke this time, okay? Not about this." She pulled his hand into her lap for a moment, tracing his fingers with hers, sizing up the differences between his long fingers and her more delicate hands. Then she laced her fingers through his and bound them together again. "These past few days—I believe you really see me for who I am now. A grown-up. A possibility. I'm not standing aside anymore. I love my sister, but Lisa didn't make you happy. I think I can. We've got this crazy chemistry thing going on, and I want to be with you in a way I've never wanted to be with any other man. I know I've thrown myself at you a couple of times to get you to wake up and notice me, us, what I think we could be, but…" Finally, she released his hand and sat back on her heels. "I will be your friend the rest of my life if that's what you want. If that's what you need from me. But I don't want to die—I don't want you to die without me saying how I feel."

"Squirt—"

"You don't have to say anything. I just need you to know that. That you're loved."

"No final dramatic speeches, okay? We're going to get through this." The girl with the stitches in her busted chin, the teenager whose pride had been shamed by a careless comment that left her weeping in her tree house didn't really know about love and the depths of what a man and woman could feel, could she? Conor reached out to free a strand of hair that clung to the dampness on her cheek. He smoothed it into to the silky waves of her hair. "It's the stress talking. Stress and fatigue and a little bit of fear."

"A lot of fear," she conceded. "But I felt this

way before Chloe's murder, before any of this happened. I never thought I had a chance with you until I saw you at the wedding. Now we may never have a chance." When Conor pulled away, she shook her head. "You don't believe me, do you. That's why you keep calling me Squirt. It keeps me at a distance, keeps you from having to think about changing our relationship." She spread her hand over his heart, and her heat seeped through his T-shirt into his skin. He felt the sad truth of her words deeper inside. "Have you been hurt so badly that you don't trust what I'm saying? Or do you still think I'm too young to know my own heart?"

Good grief, she *had* grown up. Maybe it was a woman's intuition, or maybe she knew him too well. In some ways, she had a better read on people than all his years of training had given him. She sure as hell had a perfect read on him.

He pulled her hand away and stood. "Let's just get through the next few days. Let's put the bad guys away where they belong. Then we'll sort this all out."

"I've had a long time to think about this. The decision is yours. Love or friendship? When you're ready, you let me know."

He tried to walk away. He tried to pretend he was doing some noble thing here by leaving her to her girlish fantasies. He walked out of the light from the lamp surrounding her on the bed. He made it to the doorway before his hand fisted around the carved walnut trim.

He knew she wasn't a little girl anymore. He knew she believed what she had told him. Hadn't he admitted to himself a few hours earlier that he loved her, too? She'd laid it all on the line in a way he wasn't able to. He'd spent a good part of the past few hours gauging just how serious her attachment to him was, and whether he wanted to risk a few days or weeks, or maybe only a few hours, of following his heart. If he screwed this up, he'd end up losing her forever, and that idea made him sick to his stomach. Or, he could sustain himself on the friendship they'd always shared, that he believed would always endure.

You just signed your death warrant. I'm coming for you.

The words from that last text threat played through his brain, shining a spotlight on the answer.

There was no guarantee of tomorrow. Laura Karr made him happy in ways he'd never felt with anybody else. And damn it, Conor had spent too long not being happy—not letting himself love a woman the way he wanted to because he was tired of losing people. He was tired of being the wrong boy, the wrong man. He was tired of being hurt.

Maybe he couldn't bank on forever. But he could have now. He could have Laura and her love, at least for a little while—at least until she didn't need him anymore. At least until he had to go back to Kansas City and she opted to stay in Arlington. Tonight, he was the right man. Tonight, it was safe for him to let go and love her.

"Are you okay? Can you talk to me? What are you thinking?"

Her voice drew him like a beacon from the shadows. Decision made. He turned, locked on to her beautiful eyes, and walked to the bed. Each deliberate step brought him further out of the darkness that had choked off his heart for far too long. He didn't pause except to unhook his belt and lay it and his gun on the bedside table. He braced his hands atop the bedding on either side of her, forcing her to scoot back across the bed as he kept moving forward.

"What are you doing? Conor?"

The edge of the mattress sagged beneath his weight as he brought one knee, and then the other, up and crawled over her. "Screw friendship. I want you, too."

Laura was flat on her back, her hair splayed in a halo on the quilt around her head, her hands braced against his chest. She held her breath as she questioned his intent. "So, this means…?"

Her legs were trapped beneath his, his hips nestled against her. Lying down like this, the differences in their heights didn't matter. His body was hungrily aware of each womanly curve, and her sweet scent that filled the small space between them. "I'm finishing what we started earlier. If that's okay with you."

Her hands moved from keeping him at a distance to clutching at his shoulders to winding around his neck and pulling him down on top of her. He braced himself on his elbows, not wanting to crush her. But Laura had other ideas. She bent her knees on either side of his hips. Denim rasped against denim as she cradled him between the warm juncture of her thighs.

"You know, love and friendship don't have to be mutually exclusive," she reminded him, stroking her fingers across his chin and jaw.

"I don't want to analyze this. I just want it to happen. And I pray you won't regret it."

"I won't. I'll never regret any time spent with you. I know exactly where this is leading, and I want it to happen."

His shoulders blocked the glow of the lamp, turning her eyes into verdant pools of unreadable shadow. Every cell in his body trembled in hopeful anticipation. "If you're such a grown woman, Laura Karr, then shut up and kiss me."

She did.

She lifted her mouth to capture his in a long,

leisurely kiss that chipped away at the darkness. A light turned on inside him when her lips parted, invited him to stake his claim.

Conor didn't waste any time obliging. His fingers fisted in her hair as he thrust his tongue inside to taste her welcoming heat. Her tongue danced alongside his before stroking his bottom lip. Conor mimicked the action with her, pressing, stroking, tasting. He left her lips to kiss the heart-shaped point of her chin, the tip of her nose, a trio of freckles on her cheek before coming back to claim her lips. He skimmed his hand along the curves of her hip and slender waist, bunching her sweater and camisole up beneath her arm. He squeezed a palmful of satin and lace over her lush breast, flicking his thumb over the eager tip. She gasped and her back arched, pushing her breast into his hand, twisting her hips beneath his. The feel of her body in his hands, stretching against his, was so richly, perfectly female that the most male part of him tightened in an instant response.

He trailed his lips along the rapid pulse beating beneath the creamy skin of her neck, lingering on the sexy vibration humming from her throat. He tried to pull her a few inches from beneath him, but her hair tumbled over the edge of the bed. Conor turned, shifting them both lengthwise on top of the quilt before closing his mouth over the hard pearl of her nipple, wetting her through the material, loving the shaky grasp of her fingers in his hair as she held his mouth against her to torment the responsive peak. She whispered his name, gasping against his ear as he turned his attention to the other beautiful breast.

It wasn't enough. There were too many clothes between them, too many sensations teasing his skin—cotton, denim, the unforgiving metal of his zipper, the scratchy lace of her bra—and none of them were the touch he wanted most. Groaning his unhappiness at leaving her for even a moment, he sat up, his knees still between hers. He pulled the T-shirt off over his head and unsnapped his jeans.

Laura sat up, too, her hands and lips drawn to his bare skin. His flanks trembled at the brush of her fingers. She explored the flat of his back, the breadth of his shoulders, the swell of each pectoral muscle and bicep. She dipped her tongue into the crisp hair dusting his chest and found the responsive male nipple hiding from the cool air. She laved her warm tongue around the taut bead, drawing him to rigid attention. When she sucked him into her mouth, other things sprang to attention, as well.

"Honey…" He tried to slow her down, tried to slow his own body's response to every eager touch. "Laura…"

Her response was to lift her arms and pull her

sweater and camisole off, tossing them into the darkness beyond the bed. Conor's hands were there to capture the beautiful weight of her breasts when she reached behind her to unhook her bra. When she rose up on her knees in front of him to grasp either side of his jaw and draw his mouth back to hers, he gave up on any idea of slow.

There was too much want, too much need, too many unnamed emotions arcing between them to do anything but race to the ultimate conclusion of their desire. Jeans and underwear went next. There was no talking, little thinking, only feeling as she helped him roll a condom over his straining arousal. Then Conor lifted her, laid her back on the bed and stretched out above her. He drew his thumb across her center, loving how slick and ready she was for him. He did it again, just to feel her knees clutching his hips, just to see the breathless desire for him darken her eyes.

As he positioned himself at her entrance, her head darted from side to side and she giggled. "We're upside down."

"We're perfect."

"I mean on the bed. Our feet are on the pillows…" Conor slipped inside her and she gasped. He held himself still for a moment, giving her time to adjust to his size, giving her time to adjust to this moment together, and how everything between them had changed. She looked up into his eyes, smiled. Then she hooked her heels behind his thighs and pulled his mouth down for a kiss. "We're perfect."

When he moved inside her, she held him to her body and rode the waves of the rhythm he set right along with him. The tension inside her body gripped him just as tightly until she arched beneath him with her release, gasping his name against his skin. He buried his nose in the scent of her hair and followed right after, saying her name, over and over and over.

Afterward, they quickly cleaned up and dressed again before climbing beneath the covers together. He drew her into his arms and she snuggled in, their legs tangling, her head nestling right beneath his chin, her fingers tracing slow, gentle circles over his heart.

He stayed awake several minutes after she dozed off against his chest. He wasn't ready to believe in tomorrows. But he was holding on tight to this perfect moment. Holding on tight to the woman he loved. If Laura was next on the killer's hit list, he'd have to get through Conor first.

Chapter Ten

The distant crunch of boots moving through the snowdrift outside the bedroom window woke Conor a split second before the smoke stung his nose.

Adrenaline poured through him, putting every cell on high alert, when an indistinct pair of voices joined the movement outside.

They had company.

Conor wanted another four hours of Laura tucked against his side, her hand resting possessively atop his chest before reality tore her from his arms. Hell, he wanted forever.

But reality was a bitch. And he was a cop.

And he had a woman to protect.

He rolled away from her, picking up his gun.

The voices faded as the men moved on to another location. But a peek through the blinds elicited a silent curse. Despite the dawn's winter chill, he drew his hand back from the heated glass. The haze in the room was leaking through the melting seams around the window of the old house. The men had poured an accelerant on the siding and wood trim and set it on fire.

Even though Laura was already stirring, he covered her mouth with his hand to keep her from crying out. Her eyes popped wide open at his touch. They were wary, afraid. He gentled his touch. "Get your shoes on and grab your coat."

With a nod, she scrambled off the side of the bed, sliding her feet into her boots.

She got one tied before the smoke detectors throughout the house started beeping. That meant multiple flashpoints. He'd slept too hard to notice their arrival sooner, but those boys had been busy. They were smoking them out.

"A fire?" Laura tied off the other boot, picked up her coat and go bag, and followed him down the hallway into the living room. "Shouldn't we get outside?"

He stepped into his boots and shrugged on his long coat. "That's what they want."

"Who?"

The crash of breaking glass from the back of the house drove them to the front entryway. "Them." He stretched up on tiptoe to spy through the glass at the top of the door. "Hell." He settled back on his heels just as quickly, then pushed her over to the sofa and knelt beside her. "Looks like it's a party."

More glass shattered, and Laura's fingers latched onto the sleeve of his coat. They were coming in through the kitchen. Clearly, stealth wasn't a concern for the two men. Without the walls to muffle them, their hushed voices were quite clear.

"We only have a few minutes 'til this thing flashes over. Where's the girl? Boss said to check her purse and pockets."

"Like she's gonna let us do that without a fight."

"His orders are not to kill her 'til the drive is in our hands."

The other man laughed. "He ain't kiddin' nobody. He wants that job himself. He had too much fun with the last chick. Split up."

Conor could see Laura's brain ticking as her eyes darted toward the sound of the intruders' voices. Those men knew who'd killed Chloe. He caught her chin with his fingertip and tilted her gaze back to his, warning her to focus. "Survive first, answers later." His voice was barely a whisper as he slipped his go bag over her other shoulder. There wasn't time to pull out his backup weapon, so he'd have to make every shot count. "Stay close to the floor near the front door. The fumes aren't bad here. Wait for me. Don't go outside until I know it's safe. I saw a vehicle out front, so we're surrounded. You'd be walking right into their trap."

"Surrounded? How many—?"

"Stay put. I don't want you accidentally caught in any crossfire."

"Crossfire?" She hunkered down. "What are you going to do?"

"My job."

Giving her hand a squeeze before he pried it from his coat, Conor left Laura hidden behind the sofa and moved out. The haze of smoke gathering over his head, and the darkness of his familiar boyhood home gave him a temporary advantage over the two men who were relying on flashlights to move through the house.

"Where is she?" one asked. They were in the back hallway now, going from bedroom to bedroom. Conor cut through the family room to head them off.

There they were, moving into the bedroom he and Laura had just occupied. He threw himself back against the wall, tuning his ears to their movements, readying his Glock between his hands. He recognized the two men from the night of Chloe's murder. Vinnie Orlando's entourage. More like his keepers. Faceless muscle men paid to do someone else's bidding. Probably the same two bullish thugs who'd carried away the dead body on the video.

"She ain't here."

"The bed's been slept in. Closet's empty except for some fancy clothes."

"How'd they get out?" The man coughed, then swore as a second coughing jag interrupted him. With any luck, they'd succumb to the smoke and fumes of their own making before he and Laura did. "Man, it's bad in here. No way they went out the front. And we've got all the rear exits blocked off."

The other man was already backing out of the room, on guard, unsnapping the holster on his gun. Luck wasn't on Conor's side. Time to move. "Then where's the boyfriend?"

"Right here." Conor leveled his weapon at the two men, staring down the sight of the barrel. "KCPD. They call this breaking and entering where I'm from. Put down your weapons. Get on the ground."

The two men looked at each other, laughed. The laughter set off the closest man into another coughing fit. He braced one hand against the wall and leaned into it, struggling to unhook his weapon from his belt. The second man pulled his gun, but couldn't fire in the long, narrow hallway without hitting his buddy. Conor pointed his weapon at the first man and pulled the trigger, hitting him center mass. The guy cursed and fell back on the floor. Yet despite the swearing and coughing, there was no blood. "Ah, hell."

They were wearing flak vests.

That meant he was fighting a different kind of battle. With the first intruder momentarily stunned, down with maybe a cracked rib or two, Conor raced past him, charging the second man as he raised his gun and fired off a shot.

The bullet whizzed past his ear as Conor hit the man square in the gut and tackled him. He lost his gun when they hit the floor, and it became a fight to disarm the other man. He closed both hands around the bigger man's wrist, banging his hand against the floor twice, weakening his grip on the gun. But the third blow never happened as the man beneath him struck his fist against Conor's unprotected side, knocking him off and slamming him into the wall. Now his opponent was on top of him, and it took every bit of strength for Conor to keep him from pointing that gun down between them.

Conor kicked up with his knee, nearly flipping the guy off him. But *nearly* wasn't good enough. Brute strength wasn't going to work with this guy, so Conor let go to thrust up with the butt of his hand and smash the guy's nose. With a yowl of pain and a spurt of blood, he loosened his grip on the weapon and Conor seized the advantage and knocked it from his hand.

At least it was a fair fist fight now. But where the narrowness of the old home's hallway had helped him a moment earlier, it now worked against him. This guy was twice as broad as Conor, and there was no place to roll away from him and regain the upper hand without putting himself square between Coughing Man, who was still armed, and Bruiser Boy here.

A fit of muted coughing crept beneath the grunts of the fight and the crackle of the growing flames. He wasn't the only one who'd heard it.

"Get her!" Bruiser Boy shouted the command in Conor's ear.

His buddy pushed away from the wall and lurched toward the front room. Bruiser Boy shifted onto his knee and stood, pulling Conor to his feet along with him.

"Laura!" Conor tried to warn her. But the split-second shift in focus was the diversion Bruiser Boy needed to plow his fist into Conor's chin and snap his head back against the wall. The bottom half of his face went numb, while the top half of his skull rang like church bells on a Sunday morning.

"You ain't savin' her today, lover boy." His opponent pulled back his fist.

Conor took another punch to the gut that doubled him over, but he had one advantage Bruiser Boy here lacked: a brain.

The kick to his ribs knocked him down to the floor…where he could reach his gun.

Make that two advantages.

Conor's fingers closed around the handle of his Glock and he rolled onto his back. He raised his hands and pulled the trigger, firing three rounds up beneath his opponent's vest. It did enough damage to bring the big man down.

"Laura!"

Without his own struggle filling his ears, he heard the sofa in the front room screeching across the wood floor. Laura yelped, then roared a wordless grunt. Coughing Man was after her. Conor swiped up the fallen man's gun and tucked it into his belt and staggered down the hallway. Then he heard a threat that turned his blood to ice.

"I'll kill you for that, you bitch."

Conor rounded the corner to see Coughing Man nearly doubled over, holding his gun hand down at his crotch. But that didn't stop him from clamping the other hand over Laura's shoulder as she tried to get away. Conor raised his gun, but there was no shot with Laura between them. Just as he thought he was going to be witness to the unthinkable, she raised her arms and dropped to her knees. The two go bags she'd been carrying slipped off her shoulders and fell to the floor, throwing her injured attacker off balance. As he tumbled to his hands and knees, she pushed to her feet.

Instead of running toward Conor, she whirled around, snatched the lamp off the end table and brought it down over Coughing Man's head, knocking him flat on the rug. Conor was there to pick up the gun he dropped and slide between the still man and Laura.

When she raised the lamp again, he caught it with his hand and took the weapon from her. "He's out, honey." He tossed the lamp onto the sofa that had been shoved askew in their struggle and wound his arm around Laura's shoulders, pulling her to his side. "You okay?"

Her fingers latched on to his coat and she nodded. "I'm glad your mom switched to brass instead of glass."

He smiled in relief, pressing a quick kiss to the crown of her hair. "Me, too."

A radio crackled to life from somewhere on Coughing Man's unconscious form. "Hammer. Rico." It wasn't a voice he immediately recognized. "Has Wildman been neutralized yet?" Stereo static from the back hallway indicated both men were in communication with someone, probably whoever was parked out front. "Bring the girl to me. I want to talk to her. Hammer!"

Laura pulled away, her tone breathless. "Clever name for a thug." She coughed. Her eyes were red, and tears ran down her cheeks. His own eyes stung and watered like crazy. The chemical haze was getting thicker. "We can't stay in here much longer."

Conor nodded. He needed to set aside his fear for her safety and think like a cop for a little while longer. "This guy's unconscious. You okay to touch him?" When she nodded, he gave her quick directions while he retreated to the man in the hallway to do the same. "Find that radio and any ID he's got on him. I want to know who just tried to kill us."

The bruiser in the back was dead from his injuries. Conor quickly found his radio and a driver's license that identified him as Don Urbanski. He stuffed both items into his pockets and hurried back to Laura.

She was standing with both bags hooked over her shoulders again, holding out a billfold and two-way radio. "This is Rico Martinelli. Does that name mean anything to you?"

He was more concerned about the smoke filling the space close to the ceiling. Conor pocketed the items and shook his head. Although he admired her strength on every front, he pulled his heavy bag from her shoulder and slung it over his own, ignoring the twinge of bruising around his ribcage. "I'm guessing these guys are muscle for hire. But if we can find out who signs their paycheck—or maybe who bailed them out of prison—then we can find out who's behind all this." He folded her hand into his. "We need to go before backup comes to check on these guys."

She raised her other hand to touch his jaw. Her touch was featherlight, her fingers tipped with blood as she pulled away. "You're hurt."

"Probably the other guy's blood."

"I don't think so."

He pulled her back when she tried to leave, probably to get a bandage or towel from the bathroom. They didn't have time for doctoring like that. His head was throbbing like a son of a gun, but he hadn't been shot. There were no broken bones. Couldn't say the same for these two thugs. "I'll live."

"You'd better."

Her smile didn't quite reach her eyes as he pulled her to the front door. Damn it. In addition to the black car he'd seen earlier, a county sheriff's car had pulled in behind it. "Cobb's here."

There were no fire department vehicles or flashing lights anywhere on the block. Nobody had called in the fire, and yet a cop car was here? He had no more doubts about Cobb's complicity with Chloe Wilson's murder or the cover-up of the woman's death recorded on that flash drive.

Conor immediately changed course and pulled Laura through the house to the back. But there was no escape that way, either. Originally, the flames had been localized along the back of the house. Back door. Kitchen. Bedroom window where they'd been sleeping. But those goons had poured more accelerant inside. He could already see the corners of his mother's linoleum curling up and withering in the flames.

"Conor?" Laura was backing away from the intense heat. She put a fist to her mouth, trying to stem her coughing. "It's getting hard to see, hard to catch my breath. Isn't dying in here as good as being killed somewhere else?"

Hammer and Rico's boss probably wanted to make sure the flash drive was recovered before eliminating the two people who could tell them its location. But killing them by any means was no doubt the alternate plan for these thugs who were desperate to cover up their crimes. And Laura dead under any circumstances wasn't an option he'd allow.

Conor tugged on her hand, shifting directions once again. "Garage."

They hurried out the side door through the breezeway connecting the house to the garage and piled into his SUV. "As soon as I turn over this engine, they're going to know our location. If anyone's out there, I'm running them over." He set his Glock in the center console, keeping it within easy reach if he needed it. He'd already taken the quick escape precaution of backing into the garage.

Laura nodded. "I'm ready."

"You always are." He reached over to brush his fingertip across her cheek before handing her the garage door opener clipped to his visor. "When I say *go*. Three, two, one, go!" Laura pushed the button to raise the garage door and he turned the key in the ignition. He shifted into Drive and stomped on the accelerator. "Stay down!"

The big SUV flew out of the garage, taking out the bottom slat of the garage door and chunks of paint off the roof of his car. The top of the windshield splintered with a slow-moving crack as he spun in a hard right turn out of the driveway and sped away.

He eyed the cars parked in front of the house, fading in his rearview mirror. The headlights of the cop car flashed on, and Conor braced for the chase, calculating upcoming turns and praying there were no slick spots on the asphalt from the weekend's fresh snow. But someone quickly got out of the second car and ran up to the house. The headlights went off.

The radios he'd stuffed in his pockets crackled to life. "Hammer! Rico! What the hell happened?"

He caught the first few words of an argument

before the broadcast went dead. "You should have let me handle—"

Conor turned out of the subdivision, heading for heavier traffic where he could blend in, and roads where his excess speed wouldn't be noticed, before turning on his own headlights. He glanced over at Laura's white-knuckled grip on the dashboard.

But her bloodshot eyes were fixed solely on him. "Your mother's house—all those memories. They're burning to the ground. I'm so sorry."

He reached across to take her hand. "I've got everything that matters right here."

She smiled briefly before releasing him and turning her attention to the side-view mirror. "Why didn't they shoot at us? I'm not asking for trouble but—"

"Residential neighborhood. Too many witnesses would wake up at the sound of gunfire outside."

"Why aren't they following? Are they letting us go?"

They bounced over the curb as he cut the next corner short. Conor swung his gaze from side to side, analyzing parked cars and moving vehicles, making sure his assessment of any lack of pursuit matched hers. "For now. I'm guessing there's a plan B for capturing you, but I'm not waiting around to find out what it is. My goal is to drive as far and fast as I can to get out of the metro area, and on the road to Kansas City. Trust me?"

Instead of her familiar nod, she frowned at him. As he raced up an entrance ramp onto the highway, she climbed up on her knees and leaned between the front seats to reach into the back. She unzipped his bag. "Where's that first aid kit?"

Doing his best to ignore the heart-shaped bottom in the rearview mirror, he merged into the smattering of pre-dawn traffic. "Honey, I need you to buckle up."

She plopped back down in her seat before opening the kit, taking out some gauze. "You're still bleeding." She was on her knees again, this time reaching across the console to press a wad of gauze against his chin. He winced at the pressure she used to stem the blood flow. The numbness of shocked nerves had faded. Hammer had definitely earned his nickname. He was lucky the big man's fist just split the skin, and hadn't broken his jaw or knocked out a tooth. "That's a pretty wide gash."

He waved aside her tender ministrations and held the gauze in place himself. "I got it. You sit." She reached over his lap and buckled him in first before she settled back and fastened her seat belt. He got the idea to turn on his siren and flashing lights to warn cars to pull to the right lane, so he could drive faster without endangering any other drivers. The city lights raced by in a blur for a couple of miles before he thought to ask, "Are you hurt?"

She looked back at him, reassuring him with a smile. "My throat's a little sore. Probably from the smoke and coughing. But I'm okay."

"That guy had his hands on you. You're sure?"

"After I kicked Rico in the family jewels, he wasn't too steady. He grabbed the straps on the bag, not me. I'll have a couple of bruises later, but I'm fine. It pays to be small and squirmy. He never got a good hold on me." She unbuckled again to check his wound before replacing the soiled gauze and adding strips of adhesive tape. "I think you need a couple of stitches. But I'm fine," she repeated. "Don't worry about me."

"That's never gonna happen." They hit a pothole and the vehicle lurched. When Laura bounced into the air, he pushed her back into her seat. "Enough. We're safe for now."

"How long will it take us to get to Kansas City?"

"At least twenty hours. I won't be able to keep up this speed forever."

Thinking several steps ahead of their current situation, Conor flipped on the KCPD radio on his dashboard, and adjusted the frequency to listen to local traffic reports so he could avoid congested roads and interchanges. Hopefully, he could find out if anyone was making an effort to save his mother's beloved home.

The local chatter was less than reassuring. Conor's hands tightened on the steering wheel as the dispatcher repeated the BOLO alert.

"Please be advised that the suspects are armed and dangerous." The dispatcher rattled off Conor's license plate number and a description of his SUV. "Suspected arsonists. Missouri plates."

Conor swore. "Every cop in the DC metro area is going to be looking for us with that BOLO. Be on the lookout for," he explained. "I guess that proves that Cobb is involved in this mess. He's at least on the take, covering up Vinnie's crimes."

"Where do we go if the police *and* the bad guys are after us?"

Conor rebooted his escape plan. The only thing he'd ever believed he was good at was his job. But he was really good at it. He'd always had a talent for keeping the people entrusted to him safe. And they'd been grateful. They'd all been grateful that he'd kept them alive.

His out-of-state plates and bashed up SUV would stick out like a sore thumb around here. Maybe there weren't any local cops he could trust. But that didn't mean he didn't have friends in the area who owed him a favor or two.

He took a fast turn onto Lee Highway. "I've got an idea."

Chapter Eleven

"This guy is one of the people you put into the witness protection program? Is Stephen Naso his real name?"

Exhausted from the harrowing stress of the fire and their escape from Deputy Cobb and his compatriots, Laura was running on fumes. She'd been deliciously tired after making love with Conor, and she'd slept deeply in his arms afterward. But constantly looking over her shoulder for the next threat and fearing for their lives was taking a serious toll on her energy. Still, the cup of strong coffee and fruit Danish from the used car salesman's office gave her enough strength to stay on her feet and keep moving.

Conor stood beside her in the tiny glassed-in cubicle, sipping his second cup of coffee, his tired blue eyes barely blinking as he studied the mechanics, office workers and other sales staff reporting for work as the dealership opened. She didn't think there was a single person he hadn't taken notice of on their trip here to Used Auto Bonanza, from the other drivers on the road to a group of school children waiting at their bus stop. Along with his bruised knuckles and split chin, plus whatever injuries he'd sustained that she couldn't see, that constant state of alertness must be wearing him down faster than her own fatigue.

Still, he'd never once snapped at her or dismissed her or made her feel as though she was an inconvenience or that he resented risking his life for her. He'd never complained about answering her questions about why they were here and how he knew the weasel-faced man who was helping them get a different car to drive. Of course, Conor had never said how he felt about her confession of love, either. After the way he'd made love to her and after all he'd said and done for her since the wedding, she had a feeling in her gut that he loved her, too. But was it the same kind of forever love she felt for him? Were his feelings a mix of physical chemistry and the circumstances that had thrown them together after Chloe's murder? She knew Conor had no desire to stay in Virginia any longer than he had to—there were too many bad memories here. If he associated her with any of those memories—growing up without his dad, losing Lisa, losing his mother, losing the home where he'd grown up—would he come to associate her with all the things he wanted to leave behind?

A part of her thought her sister was an idiot for letting this man go. A bigger part of her knew that Lisa never would have gotten through the chaos of these past few days, even with Conor at her side. The biggest part of Laura was glad that, at least for now, Conor was hers.

Apparently convinced that none of the men and women in the other offices or on the showroom floor were enemies, Conor crossed to the coffeepot in the corner and poured himself another cup. "It is now. If certain people knew Naso was still alive, there'd be a hitman after him," he explained casually, as if he was discussing the plot of a television show instead of a real man's erased past life. "We gave him a completely new identity almost seven years ago. Naso was my first assignment. He cooked the books for a drug kingpin down in Houston."

She shook her head when he offered to share the last of the dreadful brew. "Cooked the books? As in shady accounting? Do you trust him?"

"He understands staying off the radar better than anyone I know. He agreed to testify against his boss in exchange for not going to prison himself. Got a dangerous man off the streets, shut down one little corner of the drug trade." He set the pot down and faced her with a grin. "Not every witness I helped at WITSEC was an innocent do-or-die bridesmaid who just wanted to help a friend."

That he could find any reason at all to smile—that she was the one who'd made him smile—warmed Laura all the way down to her toes and reminded her why she'd fallen in love with him in the first place. Even if he ended up breaking her heart, she would never regret loving this good man.

After calling Thomas Watson to update him on their status and get some information on Don Urbanski and Rico Martinelli, who had indeed spent time in prison, he'd called his former boss at the US Marshals office to report the two men they'd taken down at his mother's home—if there was even a house left standing. She'd sat beside him in the car, listening to him coolly lie about the motive of those two men setting the fire and breaking in. Leaving her name out of the conversation entirely, Conor had said some fugitives from his old life at WITSEC had found out he was back in town and had paid him a visit. Although his former boss wasn't especially pleased to be awakened before dawn, he'd agreed to follow up with the fire department, to make sure they'd been called, and that no other structures in the neighborhood were in danger. He'd also agreed to send some men to the house to retrieve

Hammer and Rico if they were still there, and to contain the situation.

Then they'd gone to an ATM to pull out as much cash as they could spare from their mutual accounts and buried their credit cards in the bottom of their go bag. They were living strictly off cash and the goodwill of others for now, avoiding leaving any kind of trail that Deputy Cobb could follow until they got out of Arlington County and the DC metro area, beyond his jurisdiction and the reach of favors he could call in from the surrounding region.

The glass door opened and the balding man with beady dark eyes behind his round glasses walked in. He crinkled up his nose before heading around to the far side of his desk. "Smells like an ash tray in here. And the doctor told me I had to give up my cigars."

Laura picked up the end of her knit scarf and sniffed it. "It's our clothes. We smell like the fire. I guess we've grown immune to it. But other people will notice it, too."

"Noticing is a bad thing." Conor polished off his coffee and tossed the paper cup into the trash. He'd already put on a clean button-down and tossed his blood-stained sweater and T-shirt. But his jeans and long wool coat carried the same scent as her clothing. "I don't suppose you've got anything we can fit into?"

Stephen Naso, who'd agreed to meet them here before the dealership had opened, was a slight man no taller than Laura. He peered up at Conor over the rims of his glasses and shook his head. "I'm closer to fitting her than I am you. And she's got more curves than either of us." The older man winked at her.

"Naso," Conor warned him against the harmless flirting.

The older man put his hands up in surrender. "Hey, I'm not makin' a play for your girl. I'm just stating facts."

Conor pointed toward the sheaf of papers Mr. Naso held in his upraised hand. "Explain a few facts about the car I asked for. Can you help us out?"

"Your SUV is being torn down for parts as we speak." Naso set the stack of papers on the desk and pulled a key ring from his pocket. "Here are the keys for your new car. Gray and generic like you asked for, but with an extra kick under the hood. It'll get you where you need to go."

"Thanks." After pocketing the keys, Conor extended his hand across the desk. "You doing okay here?"

The older man shook his hand and laughed. "Who knew I had such a knack for selling anything to anybody? I'm making money hand over fist in this job. More than I ever made working in Guzman's organization."

Conor held onto his hand a moment longer to ask, "You're paying your taxes on that money, right?"

Naso pressed his hand over his heart. "This is too sweet a gig for me to mess it up by breaking the law."

With a nod, Conor picked up the go bag and Kevlar vest he'd taken from his SUV. "Keep our names off any of your paperwork. The guys who are after us have access to legal documents. I'll pay you for it when I can safely get into my accounts again."

The former witness shook off the offer as he circled the desk to get the door for them. "It's my gift to you. We're square now, right, Wildman?"

"You don't owe me a car."

"I owe you my life."

Conor nodded his reluctant acceptance of the deal and checked the main room before gesturing for Laura to follow him. "We'll talk later."

Laura shouldered her bag, but paused to kiss the older man's cheek, "Thank you, Mr. Naso. You've been very kind to us."

His skin turned a subtle shade of pink and he waved aside her gratitude. "All right. I guess I still owe you. If you ever need another favor— or a new car—call me."

"We will," she promised. "Stay safe."

"You, too, ma'am." He thumbed over his shoulder at Conor, waiting for her in the showroom. "And keep an eye on him. He's looked better."

"I will."

Naso's full tank of gas got them all the way to Pittsburgh, Pennsylvania, before Conor risked stopping to get them a proper meal. He'd made another call on one of those disposable cell phones in his bag, calling in another favor. Alice Carroll, another witness whom Conor had relocated in the WITSEC program when he'd worked for the Marshals, served them roast beef sandwiches, a delicious potato salad and gooey, thick brownies while she washed all their clothes and spritzed their coats with some scent-erasing spray, getting rid of the worst of the smoky stench. The sixtyish woman ran a catering company, but she'd called her assistant to handle the luncheon they'd been hired for so that Alice could spend the time with them. Laura lost count of how many times she thanked Conor for saving her life. And though he seemed uncomfortable with the praise, he seemed equally pleased to learn that Alice was happy, pursuing her life's passion in the culinary world instead of spinning her wheels in the business career she'd left after blowing the whistle on her former company's illegal practices.

During the lunchtime conversation, Laura also

learned that more than 18,000 witnesses had been entered into the WITSEC program, and that not one of those witnesses had been harmed or killed so long as they followed the guidelines set up for their protection by the US Marshals Service and their regional and local task forces. Laura found the statistics reassuring, Alice charming and the food delicious. It gave her a momentary reprieve from the bleakness of her situation and the danger she'd thrust Conor into. But after a quick shower, fresh clothes and a good meal, he was ready to go again.

And though it took a bit of cajoling and logical reasoning about fatigue and injuries and needing to be at his peak performance that even he couldn't deny, Conor let her drive so that he could catch a solid nap. The terrain changed from one skyline after another to a seemingly endless landscape of snow-covered hills and valleys sprinkled with evergreen trees, a few red barns and dramatic rock formations as they left the heavily populated cities and drove across eastern Ohio.

But his nap only lasted an hour or so before Conor was awake again, watching the other vehicles as they drove through Columbus, Ohio, and checking the side-view mirror for anyone looking interested in them or their nondescript sedan. "I'm glad Alice is doing well," he said after a while, assured that they weren't being followed, and that she wasn't driving too fast or too slowly or in any way that would make them stand out to the highway patrol cops they occasionally saw. He scrubbed at the stubble shading his jaw, wincing as he got too close to the wound on his chin. "She reminds me of Mom."

Laura passed the semitruck in front of them and pulled back into the right lane before pointing out the obvious. "You understand how loyal these people are to you, don't you? You may not have family, but you have connections, Conor. People admire you and care about you. Don't you ever think you're alone in this world." Maybe he wasn't ready to believe in love, or believe it lasted, but he had to understand that.

"I was just doing my job."

"They'd be dead without you doing your job. I'd be dead."

"We're not out of the woods yet."

Determined not to let that grim reminder spoil the peaceful reprieve of these quiet hours in the car, she speculated out loud about the people who had helped them today. "Alice is a widow, and you said Mr. Naso never married. Don't you think they'd make a cute couple?"

"Seriously?" His laugh went a long way to boost her own morale. "With two dead women, plus a drug-addicted artist, Cobb the Corrupt and whoever Mr. Suit Guy is—probably Marvin Boltz—after us, you're matchmaking?"

"They'd certainly understand each other—taking risks, starting new lives, keeping secrets." Did she dare push him? "I think understanding who a person really is, their history, what they need, what they fear, what they want, is a good basis for a relationship, don't you? Like Alice and Mr. Naso?" *Like you and me?*

"I think you've helped enough people for now, okay, Squirt?" *Squirt.* She understood what that meant. He was keeping his emotional distance again, maybe focusing on the job, or maybe backing off from just how close they'd gotten since Lisa's wedding. "Let's get to Kansas City and survive this first, and then I'll think about helping you use WITSEC as a dating program."

She hurt at the idea that Conor didn't trust the world enough—maybe didn't trust her enough—to give in to his feelings. But because she understood he needed to wall off his heart from his deepest emotions right now, she laughed at the joke as he meant her to and drove on toward the sunset.

She wasn't laughing later that night when she went up to the counter at the gas station and convenience store outside Troy, Illinois, just off I-70, to pay for the gas Conor was putting into the car and saw the news on the television over the clerk's head.

After twelve hours in the car, she was a little fuzzy from lack of sleep, but her eyes weren't deceiving her. That was her picture displayed on the corner of the television while the anchorwoman from a cable news station talked on the muted screen. Laura's wallet burned in her hand. That was her driver's license photo—always unflattering, but now completely horrifying to see on a TV set over eight hundred miles from home.

Laura read the words scrolling across the bottom of the screen. Suddenly, her blood was chilling as quickly as the temperature was dropping outside.

...*she is wanted in connection with the murder of two women. Unknown at this time if she has been kidnapped or is working with the man accompanying her. Officials in the Arlington area warn citizens that the man she is with should be considered armed and dangerous. If you spot them, do not approach the couple yourself. If anyone has information regarding Ms. Karr, please call this number.*

She backed away from the television, forgetting her change on the counter. "He didn't kidnap me." She mouthed the words. "We're not the bad guys."

The message played again. At least they had

the wrong vehicle description. Stephen Naso's replacement car wasn't on any official press release. Law enforcement looking for their car or license plate number wouldn't be able to identify them. But she was still there on the screen. Her picture. In a tiny town in Illinois. Across five state lines. A person of interest in two murders wanted by authorities in Virginia.

How? Why did she ever think that leaving Arlington with Conor would make her safe?

"Ma'am?" The clerk was looking at her with a strange expression on her face. "Your change?" The other woman turned to see what had Laura so transfixed. She read some of the words, looked at Laura, looked back up at the television, frowned. "Are you okay, ma'am?"

"She's tired." A strong hand clamped around Laura's arm and she startled. Her instinct to pull away vanished when she looked up into Conor's dark blue eyes. "We have to go."

"That report said you're armed and dangerous," Laura whispered.

"I am." He flashed his badge at the woman behind the counter, too quickly for her to read his name or even confirm what agency he was with. "The situation is under control, miss. No need to worry. We're running an undercover operation. We were never here."

"Okay." The clerk didn't sound convinced that

there was nothing to worry about. "Can I hear that from her?"

"I'm fine." Laura pointed to Conor and faked a smile. "He's one of the good guys."

Looking as if she thought they were both batty, the clerk pushed the money across the counter. "Do you still want your change?"

Avoiding any more eye contact with the other woman, Conor swiped the money off the counter and pulled Laura out the door with him.

"We're on the news," she muttered through clenched teeth. "Cops across the eastern US are looking for us."

"Talk later. Go now."

"How do they know about us here in Illinois?" Laura asked as Conor pulled away from the gas pump and headed back toward the interstate. "You're a kidnapping arsonist, and I'm a murder suspect."

"I miscalculated. Whoever is calling the shots is much bigger than either Cobb or Boltz." He pulled his cell phone from his coat and handed it to her. "Find Thomas's number and call him. We need answers. We need to see if he's found who Vinnie Orlando is, and why so many people are willing to kill to cover up his mistakes."

She craned her neck over her shoulder, trying to decide whether the clerk was searching for a number to call and report them, or if she'd gone back to reading the magazine she'd been perusing when they'd arrived. "I'm always going to be on the run from these people, aren't I?" She sat back in her seat and looked over at his weary profile as they merged onto I-70 again. "I can't live this way. My family can't stay away from home forever. I have a job. I have friends. I've got a whole life planned out. I'm pretty flexible, but none of this is even on a contingency plan." She reached over to grip the sleeve of his coat and the unyielding strength underneath. "You can't protect me the rest of your life—I can't ask you to do that."

He took his left hand off the wheel to squeeze her fingers. "Call him, Squirt. Once we figure out who's behind all this and expose them, either through the media or because we arrest them, it'll be over. They want to stay in the dark. They want Vinnie's problem to go away, not be broadcast or put on any police report database."

Broadcast. Laura turned her hand to squeeze his fingers before she pulled away. She was done with reassurances. She'd made a decision. "I'm going to give them what they want."

"No." Conor glared at her across the car.

But she wasn't backing down. "You haven't even heard what I'm going to say."

"I know what you're thinking. You want to meet with these people and turn over that flash drive. Then you're going to promise them that you'll never tell anyone what you saw." He shook his head, his expression raw as he glanced her way again. "One of those men, or someone they hired, beat your friend to death to cover up that video. What do you think they're going to do to you?"

"I'm not promising to keep secrets. I want everyone to know what's on that video. Chloe was right about one thing. She decided to fight for her happily-ever-after. Maybe she didn't go about it the right way, but she fought for it right up to the end. This is me fighting. I'm not going to spend the rest of my life running or hiding. Besides, Chloe didn't have you to help her."

Bless his heart. Conor was a good-looking son of a gun even when he cursed and frowned. "I'm not going to like this, am I?"

"Probably not. But I think I've got a pretty solid idea." She reached behind the seat to unzip his bag and pull out the plastic bag that held the flash drive. She turned the evidence over in her hand before tucking it into her own coat pocket. Then she scrolled through the names on his phone to find Thomas Watson's. "How connected are your friends in Kansas City? Will Thomas help us?"

"With what?"

Chapter Twelve

"She's married to a senator?" Laura sat at the kitchen counter in Thomas Watson's house in Kansas City while his wife, Jane, a registered nurse, sterilized the gash in Conor's chin and glued it shut. Laura could see why Jane had been so taken with the handsome older man, with his chiseled features and neatly trimmed salt-and-pepper hair. His easy air of authority that commanded the room made it easy to see why Conor respected him so much, too.

Thomas's pregnant daughter-in-law, Melanie, a med student, worked as Jane's assistant, taking away the soiled gauze and disposing of instruments, and preparing ice packs that none of them had been able to get Conor to use on the ugly bruises and swelling around his rib cage where he'd fought with Don Urbanski. They'd been lucky to get him to sit still, period, to have his injuries taken care of. But she learned that Mel was a gentle, patient soul, and with Laura's help, they not only got Conor's ribs wrapped with a protective bandage, but also had him holding an ice pack against his bruised flank. Of course, it helped that the Watsons had shifted their command central to the kitchen, so that Conor could hear every bit of information being exchanged, and so that Thomas and three of his four grown children—all members of law enforcement— could keep him in the loop as they made phone call after phone call to set Laura's plan for ending this nightmare into place.

She raised her gaze to Thomas, asking him to confirm the information he'd just shared with them. "Senator Webb Adams from Florida is Vinnie Orlando's stepfather. It took a little doing to get the court records unsealed—that's why we couldn't make the connection sooner. Vinnie's mother, Mona Orlando, legally changed her name years ago, probably to sever ties with her son's criminal activities before marrying the then state representative. Now she's Carla Adams. Her name's on the letterhead of a half-dozen foundations in Miami and DC. Between her charitable work and Senator Adams's political career, I can't imagine that this is the first time they've gone to extreme lengths to distance themselves from anything Vinnie has been involved with."

"You mean cover up," Conor grumbled, wincing as Jane gave him a shot of antibiotics. "Between drugs and murder, Vinnie's a guaranteed scandal."

"All the more reason to contact the press, right?" Laura still believed her plan was the only way to make the threats and the attempts on her life stop. "They literally keep their dirty secrets in the shadows. I want to bring them out into the light."

Conor reached over to squeeze her knee. "I'd still rather have Olivia or another female police officer stand in for you at the meeting."

Thomas's daughter, Olivia, was a good four or five inches taller than Laura. "Um, five-foot three? Nobody's going to pass for me but me."

"And you don't want anyone else to fight your battle for you."

Laura covered his hand with hers. "No. I don't." *Not even you, Conor Wildman.*

As if he'd read her mind, Conor shook his head and pulled away, submitting to the last of Jane and Melanie's ministrations with an impatient huff. "Don't even think about it, Squirt. I intend to be with you every step of the way."

Thomas's phone rang again. She really hadn't understood the complexity of setting up an operation like the one she'd proposed. "Excuse me. I need to take this." He patted his wife's shoulder before limping out of the room and answering the call.

Getting Conor to sit still and allow the others to help them had also given Laura a chance to know the Watsons better. She'd learned that Jane was Conor's witness in the WITSEC program that had brought him to Kansas City, and that they had grown especially close to the Watson family after relocating here. It was because of Thomas and his family's help that Conor had been able to save Jane.

Watching all this happy sort of chaos surrounding her, it seemed that Conor, Thomas and his family were going to save her, too.

She'd met Thomas's four grown children and their spouses over the past few hours since they'd arrived in the middle of the night. His middle son, Niall, had been called away to the crime lab to perform an autopsy, but she'd met him, his wife, Lucy, and their adorable toddler, Tommy, the night before when Niall had brought them a cleaned-up copy of the video, which clearly identified T. J. Cobb, Marvin Boltz and the two men who'd burned down Conor's home. There was still no ID on the dead woman, but Niall had launched a search with her general description on missing persons databases. Laura had also met Thomas's father, Seamus, and Seamus's wife, Millie, who puttered about the kitchen, making coffee and refilling plates with breakfast burritos that everyone seemed to be picking up or polishing off as they passed through to report on the results of all the phone calls they'd been making.

"All right, hon. Thanks. You and Jim be careful." Thomas Watson limped back into the room, disconnecting his call and pulling out a stool on the other side of Jane to sit at the counter. "That was Olivia. She said the precinct got a call asking for intel on you relating to an arson investigation and murder."

"I shot that guy in self-defense," Conor insisted. "There wasn't exactly time to file an incident report."

"You should do that here. Make sure there's an official record of events." He directed the information to Conor. "They wanted your home address. I sent Olivia and her partner, Jim, over there to keep an eye on things. They'll let us know if anyone shows up there before we're ready for them."

Laura set her mug on the counter. "Are you sure it's okay if we stay here? I feel bad about endangering more people."

Millie, the older woman at the stove, tutted her tongue behind her teeth. "Nonsense. It's good to have the house so full again." She carried the pot of coffee over to refill Laura's mug before she patted her hand. "I'm sorry for the cause, of course, but we're glad to have you. Our Conor doesn't ask for much. I keep trying to fatten him up, so anytime I can get him over here to eat some good food, I'm all for it."

"Our Conor?" Laura echoed, glancing over to see if he'd heard the inclusion into this big, close-knit family.

But he was focused on Thomas's phone call. "Did Liv get an ID on the caller?"

Thomas nodded. "Sheriff's department in Arlington County Virginia."

Conor swore. "Cobb. That guy's got a lot of nerve."

"He claims he's flying in to get your eyewitness testimony to events that happened there," Thomas explained. "Laura's, too. He's asking for interdepartmental cooperation."

"I guarantee you he won't be alone. And he's not getting anywhere near Laura." Conor pushed away the ice pack that Melanie was trying to secure in place and reached for the clean T-shirt one of the sons had lent him. "Does he think calling me a suspect is going to stop me?" As he stood to pull the shirt on over his head, he accidentally knocked the ice pack from Melanie's hand. When the woman with the swollen belly tried to bend down to retrieve it, Conor knelt to pick it up and hand it to her. "Sorry."

"Too much caffeine?" Laura teased, attempting to ease his tension.

"Not enough control of the situation yet."

Melanie tossed her long red braid of hair behind her back and smiled at Laura. "Let me guess, his idea of *control* is locking you up in your room while he faces down the bad guys all by himself?"

Laura grinned at the commiseration of what she was feeling. "Sounds like you've gone through something like this yourself."

A giant of a man walked into the kitchen, pocketing his phone as he bent down to kiss Melanie's temple. "She has. Can you imagine how much more protective I'm feeling now that she's carrying our son?"

Melanie reached for her husband's hand. "We don't know it's a boy yet, Tom. What if she's a little girl?"

Although Laura was confused as to why everyone called the big man Duff, but his wife called him Tom, there was no mistaking the love they openly shared. He covered Melanie's hand where it rested on her belly and kissed her again. "Oh, you don't even want to go there. A daughter? Can you imagine what kind of overprotective daddy I'm going to be? Conor gets it. The one thing we manly men can't handle is the people we love being in danger."

Conor's gaze slipped over to Laura without comment. Either he was so uncomfortable with their audience that he didn't want to reveal anything too personal, or he plain ol' wasn't ready to deal with the *L* word. "Right. Big scary daddy. I promise never to date your daughter. Did you make the arrangements we talked about?"

"Don't sweat it, Stringbean." Other than his musclebound build and darker hair, Duff Watson was the spitting image of his father. Thomas's oldest son proceeded to report on the deal he'd been negotiating with the owners of a local bar. "I've set up the meeting at the Riverboat Bar and Grill. Used to be a casino until it got shut down for illegal activities. The new owners tried to revive it as a sports bar but went belly up. I've got the blueprints for the place printing out on the computer now." He narrowed his gaze at Conor. "You sure you want something that big? That's a lot of area to try to control."

Conor tucked his T-shirt into his jeans. "It'll work for what we need. Besides, we don't want these guys to think they're walking into a setup. Cobb might buy it, but Boltz isn't stupid. He'll like the remote location."

"All right." Duff splayed his fingers at his waist, near his gun and badge. "We'll be there to back you up."

Thomas's youngest son, Keir, walked in with a

button-down shirt he tossed to Conor. Although Conor topped him in height, the two men wore about the same size, and shared an affinity for suits and ties. "Try not to get any blood on this one, okay?" After Conor thanked him for the loaner, Keir reported on his latest phone call. "Hud's a go to help out. He always likes a good party." He glanced down at Laura. "Hud's my partner at KCPD."

A knock at the front door turned everyone's attention to the entrance of the house. "Hello?" a woman's voice called out.

Keir smiled at the sound of high heels clicking across the wood floor before he moved to the kitchen archway to meet his wife, Kenna. Today, the older blonde looked more like the cracker-jack attorney Conor said she was than she had last night when she'd been playing cards with the family's eighty-two-year-old patriarch, Seamus. After exchanging a kiss with Keir, Kenna Parker-Watson turned her attention to the rest of the Watson family. "I called in the favor you asked for. My *friend*—" she rolled the word around her tongue as if it tasted unpleasant, before continuing "—Vanessa, is willing to help. Ever since she got fired from her network job, she's been looking for a legitimate story to bring her back to the spotlight." She offered an apologetic smile to Laura. "I had to promise an interview with you after all this is said and done. But she'll supply the equipment we need."

Laura wasn't looking forward to having her face splashed across a news screen again, but if she survived this, she would gladly suck it up and make an appearance. "Thank you."

Thomas spoke again, and all eyes turned to him. "I'd have been surprised if Vanessa Owen had said no to the story. Adams is on the Senate Subcommittee for Crime and Terrorism. He has access to all kinds of legal entities. That's how he can call in favors across state lines. We'll have to make sure all our ducks are in a row to make this happen."

"Will my idea work?" Laura asked. "Will Cobb and Boltz still go for the deal I proposed?"

"We'll make it work," Conor promised.

She tipped her gaze up to his. "You said my idea stunk."

"It stinks because you're smack dab in the middle of it." He brushed a lock of hair off her cheek and tucked it behind her ear. "But I haven't been able to stop you from getting more deeply involved with any of this. It's always do-or-die with you."

Thomas clapped Conor on the shoulder. "We'll make sure it's a *do*."

Laura summoned a smile. "Thank you all for helping me."

Thomas grinned. "Hey, I don't like having bad guys out there giving cops a bad name."

Keir agreed. "I don't like the idea of bad guys thinking they can run my city or country without there being any consequences when they break the law."

Duff shrugged. "I just don't like bad guys."

Everyone except for Conor seemed to be laughing as the cops and Kenna left the kitchen to study the map Duff had printed out. Melanie excused herself to use the restroom while Millie went to check on Seamus, who'd been taking a nap.

Laura was two steps away from joining the others when Jane spoke to her. "Conor's easy to love, isn't he?"

Were her emotions so readable to everyone except the tall, stubborn boy next door? "Not really." Laura returned to help Jane pack up her medical supplies and clean the counter where she'd worked. "But I do. He fights me every step of the way. He talks about losing people—I think he wants to stop what's happening between us before he gets hurt again."

"He saved my life, you know. He's like my kid brother, and Thomas treats him like another son." Jane's friendly smile faded. "But I've always had a sense that he doesn't think he's worthy of love, that he's the reason he's lost so many people. If he was a better man, a better son, a better fiancé, then the people he loves wouldn't leave." She followed Laura to the sink. "It's a little irrational, but when you've been wounded like that inside, you don't always think rationally. Your instinct is to protect yourself from being hurt again."

"He's always been there for me—as a kid, a teenager, now. My sister wasn't the right woman for him. She loved the man she wanted him to be. I love *him*—irrational, sarcastic, overprotective, caring Conor." Laura rinsed out the dishcloth she'd been using and hung it over the edge of the sink to dry. "We have history. I get his stupid jokes and he gets mine. I think the big galoot loves me, too, but he's afraid to say it. That saying it somehow makes it real. And more fragile. Can we really have a good relationship if he's always worrying about when it's going to end?"

Jane laid her hand over Laura's. "I don't know that I have the answer for you. I'm sure what you're planning for tonight isn't helping."

Laura turned her hand into Jane's, silently thanking her for the comfort. "It's the only way. Your husband and stepsons and stepdaughter all agree. I don't think I'm being particularly brave to do this. I just want my life back. I want to protect my family. I want a life with Conor. If he'll let me."

"Let's get through tonight first."

Conor reappeared, rearmed and wearing his badge on his belt now. His gaze darted suspiciously between the two women, but he dismissed whatever he was thinking and reached for Laura's hand. He walked her out to the living room and gave her one of his disposable cell phones. "You ready to call Cobb? Remember, he needs to believe that he's calling the shots."

"You'll be with me?"

"Every step of the way. I'll get you back home to your family. I promise."

"Conor…" Was that what she wanted? To return home to Arlington? Without him?

He bumped his shoulder against hers in a nudge of encouragement, misreading her uncertainty, perhaps on purpose? "Don't worry, Squirt. I'll keep you safe."

Chapter Thirteen

This was the stupidest plan in the history of plans.

Conor eyed the four men climbing out of the two rental cars and walking toward the gangplank from the parking lot onto the old steamboat that had once been the Riverboat Bar and Grill. Since the parking lot was dark, and there were no working lights on the boat, the men carried flashlights, giving off enough illumination through the bar's darkened windows for him to assess the approaching enemy. The two men with Boltz and Cobb might not be as hefty as Hammer and Rico had been, but the weapons they were packing beneath their jackets were legit. Four against two—with one of those two being Laura—weren't good odds. Bringing the hired help meant that Cobb wasn't going to pretend that he'd come to Kansas City to interview him and Laura as suspects.

He wanted the flash drive.

And he wanted them dead.

Conor carried the camping lantern he'd borrowed from Duff to the bar and set it beneath a television screen that had once broadcast Royals baseball and Chiefs football games. There were a dozen more screens around the main room, all of them dark and draped with cobwebs. A thick layer of dust coated the broken tables, stacked chairs and bar top, giving the place the feel of a forgotten landmark, frozen in time.

"Looks like their connections stretch all the way to Missouri."

Laura got up from the dusty barstool where she'd managed to sit for about thirty seconds. "Maybe Cobb brought them from Virginia when he flew in."

He supposed it didn't really matter where the muscle had come from. All Conor had to face them down was the Glock he suspected he wouldn't get to keep for very long, and the other weapons he'd hidden around the bar's interior. He couldn't guarantee that they'd be within arm's reach should he need a gun, but at least he'd have a fighting chance at evening the odds, so long as Laura didn't get caught in the crossfire.

He'd suggested Kevlar vests, but suspected those would be quickly removed, as well, before the negotiating began. He knew Thomas, his sons and several other members of KCPD were hidden on the riverboat's upper floor and in the shadows along the Missouri River bank. But that backup would be too far away if Marvin Boltz decided he wasn't in the mood to talk and started shooting. Conor breathed in deeply, reminding himself the sound equipment was all in place, and that he and Laura had rehearsed several possible scenarios for how this meeting would go.

"Do you think this place was a dump before the owners abandoned it?" She shook the curved brass railing that circled the front of the bar, rattling the loose connections to the dried wood and sending a shower of sawdust to the floor from every remaining screw hole. "Or are we going to end up dead and rotting away here, too?"

"You're not going to end up dead."

"*We're* not." she insisted. He couldn't guarantee that. Laura resumed her pacing, giving herself a pep talk in between eyeing Conor and the front door. He wanted nothing more than to take her in his arms and get her out of here, as far away from this risky game as he could. But Laura Karr had never backed down from a challenge. She never backed down from caring about a friend or doing what she thought was right. "I'm nervous. Are you?"

He grabbed her when she came close, splaying his hand against her freckled cheek and kissing her. "Terrified. But nerves will keep us sharp.

Don't turn your back on any one of them if you can help it."

She rested her hand over his and was nodding her understanding when the front doors swung open.

"Isn't this quaint." Marvin Boltz directed the two thugs who were already pointing guns at them to enter the bar first.

Cobb laughed at the romantic moment of reassurance. As Boltz set his flashlight on the bar top, Cobb and the other men walked past him. Not surprisingly, the two muscle men grabbed Conor by the arms and pulled him away from Laura. The deputy didn't waste any time putting his hands on Laura and patting her down. Conor's blood simmered as the man's big hands lingered beneath her coat longer than necessary. When she slapped his hand away, he laughed again. "Just want to make sure you two aren't wired." He turned his attention to Conor. "Or armed."

He removed Conor's Glock and tucked it into his waistband. Then the deputy straightened, grinned and slammed his fist into Conor's gut. Laura cried out as he doubled over with a whole new kind of pain blooming through his injured ribs. The only thing keeping him on his feet was the rough grip of the two men holding him.

"You ain't so tough now, are you, Mr. Detective," Cobb taunted. "Don Urbanski was a friend of mine."

When Conor could catch his breath again, he looked the worthless cop straight in the eye. "Coward."

"T.J." Marvin Boltz motioned Cobb to lower his fist and pay attention to the woman standing between them. "You led us on quite the merry chase, Miss Karr. Once you surfaced in Columbus, Ohio, we suspected you were heading here to Kansas City. But we couldn't confirm that until we got an anonymous tip from a helpful citizen in Illinois who was worried you might be in danger." He turned his dark eyes to Conor and raised a fuzzy gray eyebrow. "The woman who called thought you looked a little scary."

Cobb rolled the toothpick between his lips from one side of his mouth to the other and leered at Laura. "Why, I'd be doing my civic duty to rescue you from this dirty cop."

Her chin came up and her back was ramrod straight. "If you hit him again, I won't tell you what I did with the flash drive. I wasn't foolish enough to bring it here with me. You need my cooperation."

Boltz considered her proposal before nodding to Cobb. "He's a cop. He got handcuffs?"

Cobb flipped Conor's coat back. "Yep."

"Put them on him."

Cobb pulled the cuffs from Conor's belt and locked the first one around his left wrist. Then he smacked his lips around that toothpick and dragged Conor over to the bar, looping the handcuffs around the brass railing before securing his right wrist. He pinched them tightly into his skin and grinned before pulling away. "That ought to keep him out of my face."

Don't count on it.

"All right." Boltz nodded to the men still holding him. "You two, outside. Make sure we don't have any company showing up to surprise us."

The odds were a little more even now that the two men had left. Conor hoped Thomas or Duff or one of the other cops lying in wait would pick them up without alerting Boltz and Cobb to their disappearance. Now he could focus his attention fully on Laura, and the two men circling her.

"I don't like being inconvenienced," Boltz said, in a charming voice that had probably swayed juries in courtrooms. "You, my dear, are an inconvenience."

Too late, he saw the menace changing the shape of his smile. Conor shouted a warning, but the older man's fist connected with Laura's cheek and knocked her to the floor. "Boltz! You son of a bitch." Rage blinded Conor. He jerked against his bindings, jiggling the brass railing, the cuffs cutting into his skin. "You're all over beating up a woman. How about unlocking me and taking on somebody your own size."

"Shut him up."

Cobb happily obliged, swinging his fist and connecting with Conor's jaw. The blow knocked him back several steps and stars swirled behind his eyelids. But he quickly blinked them away, ignoring the blood of the reopened wound dripping down the front of his shirt, along with the urge to ram that toothpick straight down Cobb's throat. "Laura? I need you to talk to me."

Conor realized his momentum had carried him farther down the brass rail, closer to the gun he'd taped beneath the bar top. He calculated how far he could stretch his long fingers to reach the hidden Beretta. He came up a little short. Just a few centimeters away from rearming himself and putting down these two killers and saving Laura.

But he'd forgotten how strong that little spitfire could be. Her cheek had split open and was oozing blood. But she stood up. She snuck him a reassuring glance before tilting her gaze up to Boltz. "I'm okay."

"For now." The attorney wasn't nearly as impressed by her courage. "Where's the flash drive? Do you know how much trouble you've caused me?"

"Not as much as I intend to. Someone has to pay for my friend's murder."

"That dumb little blond bitch thought she could bargain for a proposal from Vinnie. Now you think you can bargain for you and your boyfriend's life?" The older man took a step toward Laura, drawing back the front of his coat to rest his hand on the gun holstered beneath his suit jacket. "I don't bargain. I make problems go away."

"I'm sure Vinnie's given you plenty of problems to deal with." Laura held her ground. "Did you kill Chloe?"

"I did. Now I'm going to kill you, too. Which one of you wants to go first?"

"Marv, just do it," Cobb whined, perhaps finally realizing the threat behind Conor's unblinking stare. "This isn't my home turf. I don't have the backup here I do in Virginia. Let's take care of business and get back on the plane."

"I pay you enough money to do whatever I tell you." He nodded to Conor. "Better get rid of the cop first. I can take this little one all by myself."

Cobb was smiling again as he pulled out Conor's own weapon and pointed it at him.

"Wait." Laura looked from Cobb back to Boltz. "How do you know I didn't mail the flash drive to a reporter?"

"Did you?"

"That would be very bad press for Senator Adams and his wife."

Cobb's aim wavered and Conor saw the first hitch in Boltz's cool façade. "You know about Adams?" the attorney asked, pulling his own weapon.

"I know about everything. Chloe told me some of it. I figured out the rest. With Conor's help." She looked to Cobb again. "He's a smarter cop than you'll ever be."

Boltz closed his hand around her arm and pulled her back to his side. "You don't understand a bargaining chip, do you. You've just given me one more reason to kill you and your boyfriend."

She tugged against his grip. "That's not what we agreed to on the phone. The flash drive for our lives."

"How about I take both?"

"Why didn't you take out Vinnie instead of my friend? Chloe was a good person." She refused to back down from the man who wanted to kill her. Conor began to wonder if there might be a little crazy fueling her bravery. He wondered if there was a little crazy flowing through his veins, too, because while she lectured the two men, he worked on loosening up the last screws holding the brass railing in place. "Or does Carla Adams still have feelings for her son? Is that why he gets to live and stay out of prison while the trouble around him just disappears?"

"You think you're smart." Contempt colored

Boltz's voice now. "You know what I do with women who have smart mouths?"

"You beat them to death."

"That's right. I enjoy it, too." He pointed a finger at Cobb, reminding him to keep his eyes on Conor. "Shoot him and dump him in the river."

"And risk never getting your hands on that flash drive?" Conor could play the taunting game, too. "You let Laura go. You and your goons never come near her or her family again. And I'll hand you that flash drive on a silver platter."

Laura's head swung around. "That's not what we agreed to. Conor has to go free, too." She looked back at Boltz. "The flash drive for both our lives. And know that I've made a copy. If there's even a whisper of a threat, I'll send the video to the press. Vinnie's mother and the senator won't survive the scandal. You'll be out of a job covering up Vinnie's mistakes." She included Cobb in the threat, too. "You'll be out of a job playing lackey to this bully. How do you think they'll treat a sheriff's deputy in prison?"

Cobb switched the barrel of Conor's gun over to her. Hell. She was taking this too far. "Give us the damn flash drive and I'll kill you quick, missy. Keep playing these stupid games and I'll let Marvin take care of you. Trust me, it won't be quick or easy."

Laura uttered the next words loud and clear. "There's another option."

The dead television screens suddenly lit up at the prearranged code phrase. Even through the haze of dust motes and the clouds of their warm breath in the cold air, the picture on every screen was crystal clear.

"This is Vanessa Owen with *Kansas City Secrets.*" The dark-haired reporter read her story at her desk while the video from that night in the alley played on the screen behind her. "This tidbit of gossip goes far beyond our fair city. This reporter has gotten her hands on a juicy little video. My sources have confirmed that Vincent Orlando, the stepson of Florida senator Webb Adams…"

"What the hell?" Cobb spun around, taking in the damning evidence playing from every corner of the bar. "My sources said this place was abandoned."

"Apparently, your sources aren't as trustworthy as mine," Conor said.

"Is this live?" Boltz asked, cursing at the TV screen over the bar.

Vanessa Owen was sharing the story of her career on her gossip TV show. She mentioned Senator Adams and his wife, along with the names of Boltz and Cobb, before warning viewers that the video would blur to protect them from seeing the most graphic images of their crimes. The tabloid broadcast continued with new videos of Rico Martinelli and Vinnie Orlando being arrested in Arlington in association with drug dealing and covering up the death of an overdose victim.

"Smile, Mr. Boltz." Laura took a step away from the stunned men, moving closer to Conor. "You're on camera."

Conor nodded toward the camera hidden among the junky old bottles of booze behind the bar. "We were busy today, wiring this place for sound. We just made our own video of your confession."

Vanessa Owen continued with her report on her local entertainment and news show. "Even now, members of KCPD have cornered the suspects at the Riverboat Bar…"

"Cornered?" Cobb holstered his weapon and hurried toward the door. "I'm out of here."

He quickly backed up as the doors opened and the Watsons, along with several other KCPD officers stormed in to disarm him and put him on the ground to cuff him.

They froze in their tracks when Boltz grabbed Laura and pulled her to him like a shield. He pressed his gun to her temple and retreated behind the bar, warning the others to drop their weapons and move back.

Uh-uh. Not on his watch.

Conor ripped the railing loose, and even with the brass bar awkwardly caught between his arms, he pulled his weapon from its hiding place beneath the bar and leveled it at Boltz. "Get your hands off her. Now."

Boltz whirled around, keeping Laura in front of him. "You're not going to shoot me, not with your girlfriend in the line of fire. What if you miss me and hit her?"

"You want to take the chance that I won't? I'm pretty pissed off that you hit her. So, I'm not feeling real reasonable right now."

He had to give Boltz credit for being a smart man. Realizing he was surrounded by cops and facing down the barrel of Conor's gun, he decided to err on the side of caution. He wisely set his own weapon on the bar and raised his hands. Laura shoved him away and hurried over to Conor while Duff Watson handcuffed the older man and led him out the door after Cobb.

Thomas was right there to set Conor's gun safely on the bar top and help Laura pull the brass rail from the loop of his arms and toss it away into the dust. "Where are your keys?"

"Front pocket."

But Laura was already reaching inside his jeans to retrieve the keys and free him from his handcuffs. She frowned at his wrists before reaching up to gently touch his chin. "You're bleeding again."

As soon as he was free he inspected the abrasion on her cheek. "So are you."

"The ambulance is en route," Thomas reported. Then he chided them both. "You two took your sweet time getting to the code word. I was about to order the men to breach the scene."

Laura grasped Conor's hand and hugged herself around his arm. "I wanted to make sure they confessed to everything."

"You did good, Squirt." Conor pressed a kiss to the crown of her hair. "You got the two men who were with Boltz and Cobb?"

Thomas nodded. "They never made it to the parking lot. They surrendered easily once they saw the firepower we had. The tech team recorded everything. I made sure this was a sanctioned operation, so we can use everything they said here in court. Their secrets are out. There's no hiding in the shadows for Boltz, Cobb, Orlando and their friends, anymore." Conor knew there was a reason he admired this man so much. "Besides, I've already sent a copy of that flash drive to the attorney general's office. He's contacting his counterpart in Virginia to launch an investigation into Cobb. See if there are any other investigations he's mishandled for the right price."

A uniformed officer interrupted the conversation. "Sir? Ma'am? Paramedics would like to take a look at you."

"They'll be right there." Thomas pulled out his phone. "KCPD just got a call from Senator Adams's office. He's disavowing all knowledge of what's been going on. He claims he had no idea his wife even had a son—says Boltz works for her office. I imagine a murder charge will make Boltz a little chattier about Vinnie's crimes and the work he's done to cover them up. And there's a call from your parents. Maybe you'd better fill them in on what's going on."

Laura nodded. "I will. Thank you. For everything."

"Not a problem. I owe Conor a lot. Glad I finally had a chance to return the favor." He put his phone to his ear and followed his sons toward the police cars waiting outside in the parking lot.

"It's over, Squirt." Conor looked down and brushed her bangs off her forehead. His heart hurt at the tears he saw in her eyes.

She wound her arms around his waist and he flinched at the pain that stabbed him in the side. Instead of hugging him, she switched positions and slipped his arm over her shoulders to help him out to the waiting ambulance. "I knew you wouldn't let me down."

LAURA WAS LEAVING HIM.

Conor sat on the rear bumper of the ambulance while a paramedic packed off the gash on his chin and rebandaged his bruised ribs. For nearly half an hour, she'd been in the ambulance next to him, getting thoroughly checked for any hidden injuries and holding an ice pack against the strawberry swelling on her cheek.

Camera crews had shown up in droves and taken over the far side of the parking lot with bright lights and satellite dishes and way too much talking. Some of the official vehicles still had their lights flashing, and if he listened to the quiet beneath the chaos, he could hear the river lapping against the shore off in the darkness just a few yards behind him.

They'd already given their brief official statements of tonight's incident to Thomas's son Keir, and promised to relate a more detailed report at the station on everything that had happened since Chloe's phone call back in Arlington. In fact, Keir was escorting Laura to his flashy silver sports car now. The paramedics wanted to take Conor to the ER for X-rays to determine if any of his ribs were cracked or broken. He felt exhausted, beat up and sore in places he wasn't sure he'd ever felt before.

But all that paled in comparison to the huge ache in his chest as he watched her walk away. She was going down to the precinct station now.

Tomorrow she'd be getting on an airplane and flying home to her family in Arlington. He had no reason to go back to Virginia. He had no home there, no family. He'd have a buttload of paperwork to fill out over everything he'd been involved with over this so-called vacation. What if he never saw her again?

"Hey, Squirt." His mouth called to her before his brain even had an idea what he would say. He shooed away the medic tending to him and stood. "Laura?"

She said something to Keir and turned around and came back to him. "What are you doing on your feet?" She eased him back onto the bumper and studied him with a worried expression. "I thought they were taking you to the hospital."

Now that they were relatively alone, he didn't hesitate to put his hands at her waist and draw her between the V of his legs. "I guess you'll be heading back to Arlington now. Once KCPD is done with you. Back to Ron and Leslie, your sisters, your job. It should be safe for all of you to go home now. This has been a crazy few days. A lot of ups and downs. But you can relax. Those men have no reason to come after you now that we've aired their dirty laundry." He feathered his fingers into her hair, feeling the sting of tears in his own eyes. "I'll miss you."

She framed his face between her hands. "Ask me to stay."

"Your home is in Virginia."

"And yours is here." Right. That was a problem, wasn't it? Her hands tightened on his skin. "Damn it, Conor Wildman, if you won't fight for your happily-ever-after, then I will. If you won't listen to your heart, then listen to my logic. Kansas City would be a great place to do my job. Most of what I do is online or over the phone. As far as the traveling? Hello? Kansas City International Airport? How convenient would that be. And guess what? They have these things called phones now. I think you still have two or three of them in your go bag. There are cars, buses, trains, airplanes—I can call my family. I can visit them. They can visit me here. I love you, Conor." She leaned in to kiss him. He closed his eyes to breathe in her sweet, exotic essence. When he opened his eyes, she was looking deep into his. "Ask me to stay. If you can. If you're willing to risk your heart one more time. If not… I'm sorry. I'm sorry you've given up on the fight to be happy. Because you deserve happiness more than anyone I know. But I'm not sorry that I've loved you. I will never be sorry for that." She pulled away. "There. I don't think I can say it any plainer than that."

Fight for his happiness? Fight for her? Believe

in her love? Was it really that easy? Could anything be harder?

Before he could break through the wall surrounding his battered heart, Thomas came up behind her. "Laura? Before you go down to HQ, maybe you should call your parents. I'm guessing they saw your face on the news. They called the department again, asking for Conor, asking about you." He thumbed over his shoulder to the cars and lights and cameras illuminating the parking lot. "And that Vanessa Owen is waiting to talk to you, too. Looks like a lot of reporters want a statement from you."

She nodded, gave Conor one more look, but didn't say anything. She turned and walked away with Thomas.

"Thomas, wait." Conor stopped them. He was on his feet, crossing to her. "Could you give us a minute?"

His friend smiled and squeezed Laura's arm. "Take all the time you need. I'll keep the press away."

Once they were alone, Conor pulled Laura into his arms and kissed her deeply, tenderly, thoroughly. Every touch of her lips, every inhale of her scent, every needy hum in her throat crumbled the protective armor around his heart and restored his faith in the future. "Honey, I'm sorry—"

"It's okay. I know you struggle with commitment, that you worry about losing—"

"No." He gently cupped her face. "When Boltz hit you, and you went down, I thought I'd lost you. I've lost too many people, and I don't want to lose you, too. I put a timeline on us. I was going to let you leave because…that's what people do."

"I'm not *people*, Conor. I'm your Squirt. You can't get rid of me unless *you're* the one who walks away from us." He considered that, and finally embraced the truth. He was the only obstacle to finding real happiness. "You have never left me, not when I needed you. Not once. What makes you think I won't do the same for you?"

"I'm sorry I didn't say I love you when you said it to me at Mom's house. I wasn't brave enough. Not like you. I'm sorry I didn't believe in you— in us—as much as you always have. I love you, Laura. You're my best friend and completely frustrating and totally courageous and the sexiest little dynamo… I laugh when I'm with you. I reminisce and get worked up, and it feels like it's okay to feel whatever I do when I'm with you. I haven't scared you off. I don't have to change who I am to please you. And I think you might really need me. Me. I wish I'd woken up and seen you for the treasure you are sooner."

"Conor—"

"I don't want to lose you. Not to Cobb or Boltz.

Not to my own stubborn self-preservation. I want to take a chance on us. I want to risk being happy. I'm scared spitless to do it, but I want to try. I want to love you." He touched her chin. "We've got the matching scars and everything. Stay with me in Kansas City. Marry me. Love me."

She smiled, a sweet little curve on that bow-shaped mouth that filled the darkest part of his soul with sunshine. "Well, I'd hate to waste the matching scars."

"Is that a yes?"

Laura stepped into his arms, nestling right against his heart. Right where she belonged. "Yes."

* * * * *

Look for more books from USA TODAY *bestselling author Julie Miller and Harlequin Intrigue later in 2019.*

And don't miss some of her previous titles, also set in Kansas City:

Protection Detail
Military Grade Mistletoe
Kansas City Cop
Rescued by the Marine

Available now from Harlequin Intrigue!

Get 4 FREE REWARDS!

We'll send you 2 FREE Books plus 2 FREE Mystery Gifts.

Harlequin Presents® books feature a sensational and sophisticated world of international romance where sinfully tempting heroes ignite passion.

FREE Value Over $20

YES! Please send me 2 FREE Harlequin Presents® novels and my 2 FREE gifts (gifts are worth about $10 retail). After receiving them, if I don't wish to receive any more books, I can return the shipping statement marked "cancel." If I don't cancel, I will receive 6 brand-new novels every month and be billed just $4.55 each for the regular-print edition or $5.55 each for the larger-print edition in the U.S., or $5.49 each for the regular-print edition or $5.99 each for the larger-print edition in Canada. That's a savings of at least 11% off the cover price! It's quite a bargain! Shipping and handling is just 50¢ per book in the U.S. and 75¢ per book in Canada.* I understand that accepting the 2 free books and gifts places me under no obligation to buy anything. I can always return a shipment and cancel at any time. The free books and gifts are mine to keep no matter what I decide.

Choose one: ☐ **Harlequin Presents®**
Regular-Print
(106/306 HDN GMYX)

☐ **Harlequin Presents®**
Larger-Print
(176/376 HDN GMYX)

Name (please print)

Address   Apt. #

City   State/Province   Zip/Postal Code

Mail to the **Reader Service:**
IN U.S.A.: P.O. Box 1341, Buffalo, NY 14240-8531
IN CANADA: P.O. Box 603, Fort Erie, Ontario L2A 5X3

Want to try 2 free books from another series! Call 1-800-873-8635 or visit www.ReaderService.com.

Get 4 FREE REWARDS!

We'll send you 2 FREE Books plus 2 FREE Mystery Gifts.

Both the **Romance** and **Suspense** collections feature compelling novels written by many of today's best-selling authors.

YES! Please send me 2 FREE novels from the Essential Romance or Essential Suspense Collection and my 2 FREE gifts (gifts are worth about $10 retail). After receiving them, if I don't wish to receive any more books, I can return the shipping statement marked "cancel." If I don't cancel, I will receive 4 brand-new novels every month and be billed just $6.74 each in the U.S. or $7.24 each in Canada. That's a savings of at least 16% off the cover price. It's quite a bargain! Shipping and handling is just 50¢ per book in the U.S. and 75¢ per book in Canada.* I understand that accepting the 2 free books and gifts places me under no obligation to buy anything. I can always return a shipment and cancel at any time. The free books and gifts are mine to keep no matter what I decide.

Choose one: ☐ **Essential Romance**   ☐ **Essential Suspense**
(194/394 MDN GMY7)   (191/391 MDN GMY7)

Name (please print)

Address   Apt. #

City   State/Province   Zip/Postal Code

Mail to the Reader Service:
IN U.S.A.: P.O. Box 1341, Buffalo, NY 14240-8531
IN CANADA: P.O. Box 603, Fort Erie, Ontario L2A 5X3

Want to try 2 free books from another series! Call 1-800-873-8635 or visit www.ReaderService.com.

READERSERVICE.COM

Manage your account online!

- Review your order history
- Manage your payments
- Update your address

We've designed the Reader Service website just for you.

Enjoy all the features!

- Discover new series available to you, and read excerpts from any series.
- Respond to mailings and special monthly offers.
- Browse the Bonus Bucks catalog and online-only exculsives.
- Share your feedback.

Visit us at:
ReaderService.com

RS16R